Preface

In writing t[illegible] present, in the form of a[illegible]teresting story, a picture a seafarer's life more especially of those engaged in the Commercial diving industry and security onboard shipping around the globe. The action of the story covers a few weeks in which, Divers, young, journeymen in the prime of life, and worn-out old men show the conditions working in a dangerous environment. It may be objected that, pirate stories already exist and have done for years, such a work as this was uncalled for. But a conversation with my Dive team is onboard is sufficient to show that they do not know what pirate danger means. Diving companies who to serve their own interests to mislead the divers, 'Pirates of Hormuz ' is a novel. My main objective was to write a readable story based on the happenings that have taken place over the last few years, this was the task I set myself. but whatever the verdict, the work possesses at least one merit that of being interesting and informative. There are no scenes or incidents in the story that are for real. At the same time, I believe that because it is fiction the book is not without its humorous side. The scenes and incidents are typical of the seafaring world we live in, especially the people suffering from Post-Traumatic stress disorder (PTSD.)

Chapter 1: Déjà vu.

"that feeling that one has lived through the present situation before".

John Alden, 58 years old sat in a darkened room with his hands behind his back, tied together with plastic tie wraps. Sitting there with sweat running down the crack of his arse, he began to recall similar times he had been in this kind of situation over the years. Although not as fit as he used to be, john still looked good for his age, with a firm toned body covered in black ink, the tattoos almost shinning in the dark, the eagle on his back showing the strength and power of the man, the names of Marines he saw get killed tattooed on the back of his neck. He thinks back to the 2nd of April 1982 when he last had this feeling of uncertainty creeping up on him while waiting for his captors to decide his fate.

John has lived a life training hard, working hard and playing hard, his body may not be battle ready at this moment in time and his reflexes might not be as quick as they used to be, but he was ready, ready for whatever the pirates had to give. All the training he had been through, just for this very same situation had started when he joined the Royal Marine commandos back in 1979 as a young boy. Nine months commando training down south at commando training centre, base in Lympstone, had earned him a green beret and the foundation for a career full of incidents just like this.

Memories come in floods as he sits contemplating his chances of surviving this one, he thinks back to the last time he feared getting shot, what will I do? will I freeze, will I shit myself? cower and grovel like a small child about to get a slap? now he understands why training is repetitive why they drum actions into your young mind, because when the shit hits the fan, you don't need to think, it just happens, all the drills all the knowledge all the experiences come together in a perfect reaction. This time is no different, he is still unsure of the outcome, but he knows what is going on in the background, he knows who is outside the building, he knows who has his sights trained on entry and exit points of the building.

Ten years John had served with the commandos, he knew they would be in the area, he knew how they operated, he knew the techniques they would be using right now, he knew the procedures down to the last detail. The technology may have improved but he knew the snipper weapon would still fire a 7.62 round with deadly accuracy. John waited patiently, listening for tell tail signs that the entry was imminent, he heard the chopper flying close making a diversion, he could sense the time was near when he would go deaf with the first 'Flash bang' going off and stunning his captors, the shock wave compressing the brain and affecting the hearing system for life.

The constant ringing in his ear's testament to how much damage these things do to your hearing. exposed to bomb blasts develop tinnitus when the shock wave of the explosion squeezes the skull and damages brain tissue in areas that help process sound. tinnitus is one of the most common service-related disabilities among veterans returning from combat situations. The ringing makes it difficult for john to concentrating on specific sounds around him but as he strains to hear distant sound of the town buzzing outside and the first move by the Marines.

He had made his peace with God many times in his life and never expected to reach the age he was now, he never expected to make his 20th birthday never mind his 59th but he realised now that only the good die young. He could confirm that statement after serving in the Falklands war with 42 Commando where he saw young lads die, in Northern Ireland with 45 Commando Recce troop where he saw young lads blown to bits and counterintelligence, counterterrorist operations with Comacchio Group Royal Marines before leaving the service of the Royal Marine to take up his career as a Commercial Diver.

After 10 years john left the Marines on a Wednesday and on the Friday, he was in Saudi Arabia diving in the oil rich fields just of the coast of Kuwait. While working on the seabed repairing a leaking pipeline john was told by the diving supervisor that "Kuwait has just been invaded" "How far is that away?" John asked back over the comms. "thirty miles" came back, John thought to himself, fuck! Not again. It appears trouble and conflict followed John wherever he found himself, just like now! How many times will he have this feeling of impending doom. Same scenario but different day, he recalls once standing in a deserted car park in the centre of Mexico City with a 9mm semi-automatic pistol pointing straight at his face. The policeman telling him "You are in Mexico now my friend!" in his own imitable style sounding typically Mexican. What this does to a man is incomprehensible by someone who has not been through the experience. Once again, he had that gut feeling that made his arse loosen its grip, but instinct told him he would once again survive.

John had progressed from that diver to a Diving Supervisor and onto Diving Superintendent, the position he now held onboard the DSV which had just been taken by Somalia pirates off the coast of Oman. As they boarded the vessel John thought to himself, fuck Not again! Déjà vu.

Chapter 2: The Bow Thruster

Déjà vu!

Five years ago, john had been docking the vessel for the exact same issue that they face today, the Bow thruster had frozen in a port side direction rendering the diving vessel non-operational. The Bow thruster is Indispensable for manoeuvring and dynamic positioning, Transverse thrusters are installed in the bow to improve manoeuvrability. Depending on the type of vessel, the range of application for transverse thrusters extends from brief docking and casting-off in ports or like the DSV continuous operation under extreme load conditions in demanding offshore applications with dynamic positioning. The difference this time being, when the thruster froze, no divers where in the water, so no near miss or injury. The vessel is now 10 years old and starting to break down frequently. John went to the shipyard in Thailand years ago when it was just an empty shell, so he has seen the vessel grow over the years, it's been his home, spending a total time of 5 years sleeping and eating onboard. His rotation of 28 days onboard working, and 28 days off, works out quite even, a straight 5 years!

Last time the vessel docked in Qatar where the dry-docking facilities involved a simple procedure that did not involve a two-day trip through the Strait of Hormuz, also called Strait of Ormuz, channel linking the Persian Gulf with the Gulf of Oman and the Arabian Sea. The strait is 35 to 60 miles, wide and separates Iran (north) from the Arabian Peninsula on the way to the Oman. But the show must go on. Concerning technical operations, dry-docking process is a challenge for shipowners due to the uncertainty that the Covid-19 crisis has brought. QSS are a little bit anxious about the dry-docking operations as we do not know if ships going for dry dock, will get out on time" Apart from the dry dock, critical spare parts and vessels' repair experience the same challenges. Some ships may experience operational challenges such as shipyards or dry docks closing. In addition, surveys and audits can in some cases not be conducted because surveyors are unable to attend the ships due to travel restrictions or quarantines. Maritime security continues to remain in focus in 2021, consideration of the increasing threat of West Africa Piracy, concerns to shipping in the Straits of Hormuz and Arabian Gulf due to tensions, and random piracy.

The Technical superintendent is to Prepare the vessel for dry-docking activities and Prepare vessels for dry-docking by coordinating with dry-docks personnel and perform repairs with increasing global travel restrictions, many clients are finding Oman Dry-Docking supervision services to be of huge value. Many simply cannot mobilise their own pool of Superintendents to attend their vessels for critical dry-dockings and repairs Their Dry-Docking Services invaluable because QSS cannot mobilise their own Superintendents to attend the vessel. locally resident Marine Surveyor network is vital during this time, enabling surveyors' onboard ships where travel between countries even cities is limited or non-existent. Dry dock supervision services are designed specifically to protect interests and to ensure the dry-docking is well-planned, controlled and executed in line with industry best practise and with minimal cost-escalation. Critically, ensuring that spending authority is respected, and financial exposure is minimised where possible. Whilst ensuring that asset-integrity, longevity, and fulfilment of future charter commitment is not compromised docking services are available globally, with a particular strength coming from Oman operates a fully-manned operational centre in Qatar.

John and the lads do not really enjoy dry docking as it involves a lot of chipping and painting the dive system, along with boredom setting in while the vessel is turned into a workshop with people swarming all over the ship, each with specific jobs and tasks to complete. The dry dock has a very pungent smell of dead marine life as the hull is scraped clear of a few months' worth of marine growth and the smell of new paint. The biggest problem the divers encounter is they must stay dry, this break in routine becomes uncomfortable and starts to effect the moral and mental state of the divers. No one was looking forward to the docking, especially in an unfamiliar country. The most complaints John received before the sail south was "what about the internet?"

The internet has changed offshore life beyond recognition, John remembers life on the construction barges where the only communication with home was via a written letter, which would take anything from two weeks to a month to arrive onboard. Now the divers had instant messages bringing problems from the outside word, problems John had to deal with especially when it comes to people wanting to get off the job by using a death in the family excuse. They would walk into his office with the droopy eye look, attempting to look sorrowful and tell john that "my mother is in hospital with only days to live, I need to get off home right now!" John had heard it all before but had to play the game and get them off as soon as possible. Nine times out of ten the diver would have a better job offer, one that did not involve a month in a dirty dry dock facility with no air conditioning and days of uninspiring work, who could blame them thought John as he arranged transport to get the diver off the vessel, "Black hawk down" was the cry from the remaining divers onboard.

John as the Superintendent was always fighting fires in a metaphorical sense, he was the boss he was the father, the mother and everything else for the dive team, he was the councillor the psychiatrist and the agony aunt all in one. Most of the divers come from a military background so you would expect them to fend for themselves when it comes to requests from management, but they don't, its "John can you do this" or "John can we do that" god's sake john would shout, but then he would do it! he loved them all really and would do anything for those divers.

Chapter 3: The Strait of Hormuz

"Though I walk through the valley of the shadow of death." Yea, though I walk through the valley of the shadow of death, I will fear no evil: for thou art with me; thy rod and thy staff they comfort me.

The Strait of Hormuz, located between Oman and Iran, connects the Persian Gulf with the Gulf of Oman and the Arabian Sea. The Strait of Hormuz is the world's most important stretch of water when oil is in demand. Today, there are several hot spots for modern piracy including the Gulf of Aden, off the Somali coasts. Piracy defined as "the act of boarding any vessel with intent to commit theft or any other crime, and with an intent or capacity to use force in furtherance of that act". In simple words piracy is an act of robbery or criminal violence at sea through illegal use of force by non-state agents, popularly known as "Pirates". In recent years, the problem of piracy has emerged as a major threat to sea transportation in some parts of the world. position and time of attack, consequences to the crew, vessel, and actions taken by the crew and coastal authorities.

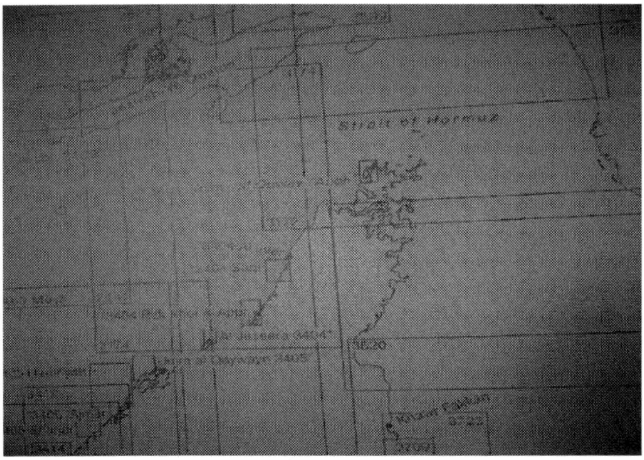

Strait of Hormuz chart.

The Strait of Hormuz. There has been brutal hijacking of ships off the Muscat coast by Muscat pirates, which grab the global media headlines. The Strait of Hormuz remains a hot spot for piracy today, but in recent years, the area has seen a dramatic downturn in piracy due to coordinated patrolling by navy forces, and increased level of onboard security on vessels. piracy in the Indian Ocean is getting more lucrative and more violent, despite an anti-piracy EU naval force patrolling the area. Like legendry pirates, modern pirates are still involved in looting and hijacking ships for ransom, but their ways of operations have dramatically changed over time. Modern pirates now don night-vision goggles; carry AK-47s, heavy machine guns, and rocket launchers; navigate with GPS devices; and use sophisticated speedboats mounted with heavy mortars to target ships. Pirates are attacking ships with Russian made 82 mm mortars that can target a ship as far as 5 kilometres from shore. Modern pirates today are part of organized crime gangs that target big and small cargo vessel Piracy in the modern era takes a quite different form, in regions where “weak states” are easily corruptible and scarce economic opportunities in legal forms of work make piracy an appealing alternative. Pirate attacks largely occur in a few “hotspots” around the globe and are driven by several factors ranging from corruption and institutional weakness, a lack of economic opportunities the major hotspots for piracy in Gulf of Aden. There is a connection between individuals that are part of non-state violent groups, kind of rebellious groups, plus in Somalia the police or people dressed as police. so, members of these groups that are fighting against the state are also engaged in piracy as well, such states have a hard time addressing problems with piracy because they are economically weak and lack the resources necessary to adequately challenge pirate attacks. Furthermore, large populations of people suffer from poverty and joblessness, which often makes piracy one of the few economically viable lines of work.

Never has there been a void in pirate attacks on the seas, but pirate activity has slowed. Blackbeard’s, Captain Kids, and other one-eyed, hook-handed robbers who plundered ships of yore. the role has been filled by angry young men carrying guns, rifles, grenades, and missiles. these pirates seek to act as modern-day Robin Hoods, distributing wealth from the hands of the rich to those of the poor by capturing vessels and holding onboard personnel for ransom. pirates today evoke the same fears as they did in ancient times. And they strike far more often than most realize. The DSV had concerns currently pertaining to the strait of Hurmuz and the Somali Coast. Piracy warnings in place as they departed port.

John and his team have prepared for many challenging scenarios, and the ship is well-equipped to handle situations if pirate’s attack. the difference between an act of terrorism and piracy, it is a crime of piracy when an act is committed within international waters and, thereby, outside the territorial jurisdiction of any given nation. Waters become international past the 12th nautical mile of territorial jurisdiction, and the prescribed Maritime Safety Protection Area is lawfully patrolled by international anti-pirate taskforces. But there's distinction between piracy and terrorism. Piracy takes place when the motive is strictly for financial gain; pirates try to board ships with the intention of robbing them or holding the crew or passenger's hostage for ransom. when an attack is for religious or political gain, the term terrorism is used. Pirates do attack vessels and oil tankers, The Diving support vessel on its way to "Dry-Dock" that passes through the Gulf or other high-risk areas, what is the likelihood that pirates will attack, not likely thought John. Another vessel attempted the journey a week before and was about 100 miles off the coast of Oman when pirates fired AK-47 machine guns and rocket-propelled grenades to highjack the ship. The ship was hijacked; crew members were ultimately rescued, and the ship was recovered after a ransom was paid.

Compared to the sheer quantity of commercial ships moving through the area and since incidents impacting vessels and oil tankers are clearly more common there are no laws on the books to force shipping company compliance, the International Maritime Organization does suggest tactics, techniques and technologies that offer interesting tips for pirate-attack evasion. Ships should have a security plan that anticipates an attack by pirates. "Planning and training must be on the basis that an attack will take place and not in the belief that, with some luck, it will not happen." Officers and crew are asked to rehearse elements of the plan.

Early detection of a possible attack is the most effective deterrent. Tools to offer advance warning include, among others, "low-light binoculars, radar that detects small crafts, night vision devices and barbed wire. "Ships should travel with lights blacked out, except for mandatory navigation lights, turning on the ship's lights as attackers' approach could alert them that they have been seen, dazzle them and encourage them to desist."

The use of Long-Range Acoustic Devices. Primarily used by warships, they serve as a long-range hailing and warning, directed acoustic device, designed to communicate with authority and exceptionally high intelligibility in a 15-30-degree beam, it's a device that sends sonic waves out to a target, and the resulting din can cause eardrums to pop and bleed, which stuns the criminals. Water pressure of 80 pounds per square inch from a powerful hose can deter attackers. Another tactic? "Provided that navigational safety allows, masters should consider 'riding off' attackers' craft by heavy wheel movements the effect of the bow wave and swash may deter would-be attackers. Onboard the DSV officers are encouraged to carry firearms. The rationale Carriage of arms onboard will encourage the old saying "Carry a knife, take a life"."

When it comes to piracy, ships are prepared for defence in several ways. On any given sailing, whether in known piracy waters or not, ships monitor movement in the area. The DSV did contract maritime information, research and tracking companies Global Marine Networks, LLC. This organizations keep ship owners abreast of happenings at sea. They also have the complete ability to track vessels and can show any change in planned itineraries or signs of distress. Other efforts by vessels to protect crew include vigilant lookouts by officers and crew members for suspicious movement in the water, as well as consistent viewing of surveillance cameras. Bright spotlights are used for lookouts on dark nights and to help ship officials spot approaching boats. All of this occurs even when pirates are not sighted make sure all the are aware of these tactics.

As the DSV was approached by pirates a whole range of tactics. Employed like crew members assist in the use of fire hoses onboard defence devices to divert the perpetrators from boarding. The behind-the-scenes training that officers and crew receive is intense. Piracy attacks and terrorist attacks are treated equally. The lines of communication between ships, office personnel and government authorities are constantly open. Regular crew members go through weekly drills for safety purposes, while trained experts are contracted to be onboard in case of an approach. These contractors are trained by their respective companies and bring that training onboard. Each crew member has role to play in an emergency. Just as there are updated information and training programs for fire safety and weather precautions, there are always updated classes on operating new devices and technologies. Most Divers will go through their careers at sea without ever needing to use that training and knowledge -- but most is not all. Crew members are trained to act in an emergency, but little is publicized about the actual security crew that all ships employ. Most of the DSV crew have had serious defence training, that comes from military experience, they're sourced from the UK and they are already well trained before they even step onboard.

One Diver, his military training, which began at age 18 in unsafe areas of the world enabled him to prepare for any scenario, as he had already seen the worst in people. He was walking the deck one night, while sailing the Straits, and heard a slap and banging sound along the ship's side. Walking toward the sound, I found a boat that had successfully hooked a rope on the aft railing. When one of the attackers spotted him, he started shooting. Members of the security team immediately started throwing heavy objects at them. They also called for backup. The others arrived within minutes and started shooting back at the unexpected pirates, who had avoided the thrown objects up to that point. Dodging bullets was another story, and security held them at bay. The total event took 20 minutes to end.

Some support is available for ship operators in troubled waterways. The U.K. and other countries have beefed up security for vessels around the busier areas. They often work together to keep ships safe; it's more common now to see vessels steaming through the Gulf, Navies from various nations, as well as NATO and the European Union have all shared in the patrolling duties. The coronavirus weakens nations, economic fallout from the coronavirus pandemic poses severe challenges for countries with few resources and weak governments. West African countries already struggle to police their territorial waters. This region has not yet been severely affected by the coronavirus, though infections are growing. As hospitals fill with COVID-19 patients, the regions' governments, shift their public safety efforts away from sea piracy and toward more immediate concerns on land. This will create opportunities for pirates. The disease has made it harder for crews to protect ships. Most vessel crews are already stretched thin. If crew members get sick, restrictions on international travel prevent their replacements from meeting the ship in whatever port it is in. around the globe, less trade and low oil prices, brings less revenue for shipping companies to spend on armed guards protecting ships against pirates. As a result, ships will become easier targets for pirates. Poor economic conditions around the globe make ships look like easy targets, desperate people turn to piracy, and ramp up their existing efforts to survive.

Governments just do not have the capability of going out and addressing this problem," "They do not have enough personnel and they do not have enough vessels, be it Coast Guard or naval vessels. These states tend to be corrupt as well ... That certainly applies to Oman, which is both a weak state, but also a nearly defenceless state. In early January, eight armed raiders boarded the DSV as it entered the port. They fired warning shots toward the ship's bridge, boarded the ship and opened several rooms, removing items before escaping in two speedboats.

The Oman is a hot spot of global piracy, armed robbers regularly attack ships in and around the port. It is the seventh-busiest port the gulf, handling most of the Middle East's industrial imports and exports. Ships moored along the port's quays or, like the DSV, transiting its narrow river passages are easy prey for local criminal gangs. Only a few short years ago the international community was celebrating the end of maritime piracy. Worldwide in 2019, there were fewer attacks and attempted attacks on ships than there had been in 25 years. However, as the DSV attack hints, pirates are getting more active. Already, the first month of 2021 we seen an increase in pirate attacks and attempted attacks, over the same period in 2020. Modern sea piracy often involves pirates in small fast boats approaching and boarding larger, slower-moving ships to rob them of cargo, crew valuables, communication equipment to seize the ship and crew for ransom. Crisis Management, International Ship and Port Facilities Security, Security Management, Maritime Intelligence, Vessel Safety, and Marine Security (ISS) is a Specialist Business Risk Management Security Consultancy, based in Singapore. with a global operations range from the UK, and the Middle East, Africa and the Asia Pacific region. This company formed by one of Johns mates when they both served in the Royal Marines together "Recce Troop 45 Cdo". Sooty was an old friend of johns, he remembers the time years ago, while training a small group of Special forces candidates in the United Arab Emirates, one of his men had tied off his rebreathing apparatus onto one of the SBM chains before climbing aboard the tanker for a rescue operation. Afterwards when the exercise had finished and they went back into the water to recover their equipment he discovered the kit had gone, lost! Sooty found John on his DSV and asked him to recover the gear with his divers the next time they did maintenance on the SBM PLEM. They never did find the rebreather which cost around £5000, "lost but not forgotten" John used to quip.

Chapter 4: Security

The cooperation of navies from around the world promises high tactical value for the ships, aircraft, and divers involved, while demonstrating international resolve in defending maritime security against potential threats.

It is one thing to ward off Somali pirates. It is another to tackle the Iranian Revolutionary Guard. The maritime security industry has experienced a flood of demand from shippers spooked by attacks on tankers in the Gulf of Oman, which the US and UK have blamed on Iran. They have been flat out and have deployed an additional 70 guards in the Gulf since the attacks last week, the security firm UK-based Ambrey, which over the past decade has become the largest provider of security personnel to ships Mr Thompson expects the number of security guards deployed on vessels to increase by approximately 25 per cent in the coming weeks, based on the number of inquiries Ambrey has received. It represents a welcome boost for the industry, which has experienced a lean period as piracy off the Horn of Africa diminished over the past few years just as an influx of cheap labour drove down costs. The cost of hiring a team of three or four guards for a 12-day journey has dropped from the industry peak of $40,000 to well less than half that level. One executive said that previous pricing "wasn't sustainable". Now guards on ships have become a "commoditised service". "It's not the rock star days that it used to be," , a risk consultancy that advises a number of major shipping companies When pirate attacks off Somalia became commonplace last decade — inspiring a Tom Hanks film detailing the capture of the Maersk Alabama cargo ship, the number of security firms offering guards proliferated, often founded by ex-special forces or other elite military personnel Guards were generally drawn from the ranks of elite military units in the UK — usually former Royal Marines, Parachute Regiment, or ex-special forces soldiers such as those that have served in the SAS or SBS. Franks, a former private marine guard, said that at one stage the high pay meant the Royal Marines were "haemorrhaging" men attracted by what amounted to a cash-lined bridge back into civilian life. Many found the life testing. Conditions on ships can vary widely: some modern cargo ships are equipped with gyms and high-end canteens while older vessels are often basic at best, with guards facing a lottery every time they are deployed. Ryan, a former Royal Marine who worked as a guard for two years, said that to be assigned to a Greek-run vessel meant "you knew you would eat like kings". A Chinese-run ship, on the other hand, "often required a strong stomach". Increasingly, guards are now lower-paid Asian or eastern European contractors who command far lower rates. Ryan said that the level of specialised guard training has improved in recent years because of increased industry regulation and the fact that former marine security officers have set up centres to prepare recruits. But the changing demographic meant the average guard does not arrive with as much experience as five years ago. "Now a lot of the guys going into the industry are from India and Nepal instead," said Ryan. "They're brave," he added. "But Nepal is a landlocked country." John who spent four years as a private maritime security contractor, said that increased competition had already driven consolidation across the industry. He estimated that it would soon be whittled down to just a "handful" of major companies. "Around 2011 or 2012, there were about 460 private maritime security companies," "But many have gone missing in action". Some companies have thrived under the new conditions. Ambrey, which many in the industry say helped drive down costs when they launched nine years ago, has increased turnover from £26.1m in

2016 to approximately £50m in 2020. "It was a frothy market five years ago," said Thompson. "But it's gone through a natural evolution." The tense situation in the Middle East might not return the industry to the boom times but it does present welcome demand, as well as specific challenges. Guards deployed in the region tend to be unarmed: opening fire on elite state-backed forces is considered unwise, even in self-defence, while the rules on carrying firearms vary from country to country in the Middle East. But trained guards can improve the quality of lookouts onboard, providing extra manpower and utilising specialist equipment like night vision googles, helping sight potential attackers early. The nature of the attacks, which is still being hotly debated in maritime security circles has also complicated the response from shippers.

For the attack on the DSV, the UK have accused Somalia of being behind the attack, piracy guards are normally tasked with deterring. "We still don't know for certain what kind of threat shippers are facing," he said, adding there was still debate over whether the vessel had been attacked "In the circumstances, improving procedures on board, from monitoring the vessels both in port and at sea, ensuring the crew know what to do in the event of an attack, dusting off crisis management procedures at corporate level, may have more benefit than putting guards on board." Maritime security experts said clients with tankers in the region could consider several measures, from trying to ensure they travel in daylight through the Strait of Hormuz, the narrow choke point separating the Gulf states from Iran where approximately 20 per cent of the world's oil flows every day, to sailing at maximum speed. JC operations manager said the company would "consider all possible measures to ensure the safety of our crews and vessels". The mystery has complicated the response. "We are not confident of who or what is executing these attacks," said Ben, at Maritime Asset Security and Training, which has provided guards to at least one vessel in the region. "If this is being done by Somalia, they need to maintain deniability." Where possible we actively engage with clients early on in their gap analysis, supporting them through a Project Security Risk Assessment and identifying risk exposure. This allows us to explore both opportunities and constraints, quantifying a proportionate response to specific threats. We also work closely with our local contacts to determine key legal requirements and contextual challenges. We can then write a bespoke security plan, covering all the areas of risk.

Then deploy a specially selected security team to deliver the physical security service on the project itself, supported 24/7 by operations management staff in the head office. Those security services could involve anything from providing armed security on board or hiring and managing local armed guards, to offering unarmed guarding and management of the vessel, experienced at providing post-incident support, on vessels post-hijack, assistance to ransom deliveries. The DSV had a team onboard they had not been hired for the journey through the strait of Hormoz, they were the dive team. The team comprised of three former Marines, two former Royal engineers and three ex clearance Divers from the Royal Navy and one ex foreign legion guy. The DSV was in good hands when it came to security, these guys had seen combat.

Big Pete, called "Big Pete" because he had a massive cock! With his expertise of firing explosive charges underwater and the Royal Engineers history as they became responsible for harbour defences, using submarine mines in conjunction with searchlights. Indeed, the Submarine Mining Service grew into a major specialization and was not handed over to the Royal Navy until 1905. Operational diving was introduced in 1839 and Royal Engineers became involved in flying at the time of the American Civil War. This speciality led from balloons, airships, and man-lifting kites to powered flight and the formation of the Air Battalion Royal

Engineers which became the Royal Flying Corps, precursor of the Royal Air Force in 1912.Jack of all trades good blokes to have onboard. Lofty belonged to the 1st Foreign Engineer Regiment (1er REG) of the French Foreign Legion. The 1er REG is specialized as the regiment engineer-amphibian. Because of its specialization, the 1er REG has its own platoon of elite combat divers, Plongeurs de combat du génie Engineer Combat Divers.

Lofty the legionnaire was mad a bag of mad snakes but would lay his life down for all the team, he was dependable and experienced in all areas of security and counter terrorism. It is the dark romance of the French Foreign Legion: haunted men from everywhere, fighting anywhere, dying for causes not their own. Legionnaires need war and there is always a hopeless battle somewhere in the world. Lofty the diver was about to find his onboard the DSV.

The two Former Clearance Divers onboard had both, worked in arduous conditions conducting bomb and mine disposal during Operation Corporate in the Falklands in 1982 and in the Red Sea during Operation Harling in 1984. In 1987, they cleared Iranian mines in the Gulf of Oman and in the Persian Gulf during Operation Cimnel. In 1991, they were back in the Persian Gulf during Operation Granby, this time clearing hundreds of Iraqi mines laid off the shore of Kuwait, so plenty of experience there, they had forgotten more than most had learned!

Chapter 5: The Sail

"Enthusiasm is the steam that drives the engine."

John the Diving Superintendent (Former, Royal Marine Commando) onboard the Diving Support vessel (DSV) had to go for repairs in Oman. A team of 16 Divers and 4 ROV crew plus Marine crew made the vessel total 60 people onboard, the vessel was 70 metres long with a top speed of 12 knots. It was 2021, the evening of February 23rd. It is a night that John will not forget. He did not need photos to remember that night anyway. Everything is as clear as a bell. They were in the Arabian Gulf. they were on the way south from the port in Qatar. Their transport the DSV. This certainly was not the customary routine job for the Divers onboard, but nothing was moving forward in a customary manner. They had been ushered in secret out of the country Obviously, there was no time to wait. John was on the back deck having a smoke, one of the rare moments he managed to steal away by himself. he remembers watching the sunset off the ship's starboard side when he heard a song come on the radio. Until the moment that song came on, he had been completely oblivious to the presence of music. It is funny how a familiar song brings a distant moment into precise focus. Somewhere on board the DSV, He heard, "Don't Let the Sun Go Down on Me" by Elton John. No shit, he said out loud. No shit! An old favourite song had suddenly been filled with new meaning. John had got the job onboard the DSV earlier in the winter. A stretch in the Middle east seemed as good as any to spend a year diving. It was a secluded place, far away from any distractions. He wanted to improve his skills and get into shape and the best condition of his life, he thought. he wanted to get a steady rotation on a Diving contract. He also had an eye on saving a little money. With all the diversions back at home, saving money proved to be a bit challenging. No one in his family had ever gotten ahead of the game. A one-year contract in the Middle east, away from any temptation to splurge, seemed like as good a place as any to stock away a few pounds. As the team prepared for the journey to Oman, none of them knew about international tensions in the area. No one knew what was brewing between the governments of the area. None of them knew a thing about crumbled talks at the United Nations, and none of them really had to. As the date for departure crept ever nearer, all any one of them saw as challenging was the prospect of spending two days on the sail down to the Oman for Dry Docking.

While traveling at approximately 12 knots near the Straits of Hormuz, 3 small Somali fast boats that approached the ship at high speed at a range of just under two nautical miles, before the Iranian vessels were even visible to the naked eye, watch system automatically identified and tracked the inbound vessels as potential threats. The system accurately identified each vessel's bearing, range, heading, speed, and estimated time to intercept the ship. Watch system assigned a threat probability to each incoming vessel, and as each vessel exceeded the system's attack probability threshold, they identified it as a threat. automatically engaged the dominant threat (i.e., the one with the highest threat probability), and began recording the incident digitally and with video. without human intervention, watch system directed its pan/tilt unit to swing around and direct its countermeasure against the vessel posing the highest perceived threat to the ship. Meanwhile, watch system continued to track and assess the other 11 vessels. When the leading Iranian skiff passed within 100 meters of the ship's bow and began to move away from the ship on its starboard side, watch system automatically instructed the port side pan/tilt unit to swing around and engage the highest probability inbound threat that remained. This process was repeated until all 12 wooden skiffs passed at high speed from the port to the starboard side of the ship protected by Watch system. Using our system's built-in, automatic digital and video recordings of any threat incident, they were able to easily re-create the "Swarm" and system's response. camera and radar display showed on the ship's bridge during the actual event.

visible on the radar display, the system had automatically identified and tracked the inbound vessels as potential threats. It has assigned a threat probability to each vessel and has automatically directed the port side pan/tilt unit (and related video camera and countermeasure) to engage the most threatening skiff. The dominant threat, vessel #3 turned bright red, while the remaining threats are shown in pale red. The boat posing the dominant threat is always visible in the centre of the port side's video display.

All the Divers abandoned their rooms at roughly 02:00 hours on the evening of February 23rd. Within minutes, the accommodation was empty. Captain Ram, a former Indian Navy captain, would not give up his vessel easily. He took his bridge crew and the hand full of Marine crew and fled to a safer location. As the divers led by John moved out to firing positions, the vessel became the temporary base of operations for defence of life. Each of the teams designated for a specific position at a different defensive point on the vessel. Intelligence had led Captain Ram to the belief that the pirates spotted would go straight for the bridge away from the deck. As an attack point, seemed a natural start, but the deck was also of tremendous strategic value. If the pirates could secure the area, they would have control of the vessel, to further secure their foothold, so the divers defences were spread out accordingly. Gas cylinders were set up in the deck tunnel; they would render it all but useless for the pirates to enter the accommodation. A few men were situated directly above on the deck; a machine gun team set up, weapons trained on the waters, which seemed a likely landing place for the pirates. Team one with John placed a short distance from the bridge wing port side. The half dozen divers stacked up along upper decks, this position armed with an 84mm anti-tank weapon and 66mm anti-tank missiles. There was a nearby lifeboat; their orders to delay the pirates for as long as possible before eventually falling back into a secondary position. team four was also armed with an 84mm anti-tank gun and they slotted in on the opposite side of the vessel on the starboard side, ready to take on any pirate craft, or whatever boats would attempt the tight passage through the narrow entrance. They were ready to engage with Somali invaders should they approach from the south. An observation point was set up on bridge. Only one Diver was sent up there to keep watch. His name was Mike. Mike would keep an eye all around, and if he saw anything, his orders were to sound the alarm. When all the divers were finally in place, the dory was launched. The work dory used is of Aluminium construction with a total length of 8.1m and a beam of 3.2m which is large enough to accommodate a team of 7 divers in comfort allowing sufficient room. The Dory is fitted with an appropriate means of propulsion with 2 x Yanmar D36 Diesel 36hp outboard motors that will allow it to return to the support vessel in any reasonably foreseeable weather conditions in a time not exceeding 15 minutes. Equipped with radar, it would keep watch over towards the dark waters to the north. they use radar for Navigating. in the fog is impossible without radar Offshore, they can locate small boats, and obstructions. Solid-state radar provides better target resolution, even at an amazingly close range. Docks, channel markers, moored vessels and other critical targets are displayed with clarity and separation, for added confidence in close quarters. Solid-state, broadband technology also eliminates the "main bang" of a pulse radar the obscured "dead zone" immediately around the vessel which interferes with close target detection.

Shipboard life ends up being a lot about waiting around. Hurry up and wait. Ninety-nine percent of life is quite tedious, spent lingering on word. Get into position and wait. As the morning of February 24th crept through the anxious small hours, every one of the vessels did precisely that. They waited on word of engagement with the invaders. Then, finally, that word came down. It was

02:30, only a short half-hour after leaving the accommodation, that their eyes in the sea, the Dory, detected the approaching enemy; by 03:30, it was obvious that a significant Somali force was manoeuvring to the north. An hour later, Mike saw the fast boats approaching the vessel. Word began to spread like wildfire throughout the crew. The pirates were dressed as police. There were three of the impressive American-made fast boats, each loaded with men and equipped with .30 calibre machine guns. The 20-man invading force moved slowly up towards the vessel before breaking off into two separate parties: the first moved to the bow, rounding back behind the stern, while the other headed directly toward the rescue zone, where they made their first, vicious attack. By a little after six in the morning, the pirates had been hopeful of catching the crew sleeping. They saturated the structure with heavy machine gun fire and phosphorous grenades. The attack was successful in destroying the structure, but they had arrived too late. If the attack had come any earlier, the result would have been devastating.

The Crew had been successful in avoiding devastation on the bridge, but by now, John had to recognize what was going on. The Marine forces were outnumbered and badly outgunned. The guys had managed to pick off one of the fast boats A sharp-eyed marine managed to get off a shot from an anti-Armor weapon, striking the control console. Others opened fire on the boats stopping it in its track. They may have slowed down the advancing pirates, but this only served to make things worse. A boat of pirates emptied their men onto the main deck, giving them cover as they moved forward, machine guns blasting. As dawn crept closer, skirmishes like these broke out all over the vessel. The Divers fiercely engaged the pirates. The determined men fought as long and as valiantly as they could. Backs against the walls though, each movement seemed to send them scrambling for a new position while the pirates gained deck by deck. Scattered gunfire was exchanged between the crew. Here and there, a lucky sniper caught one of the divers, racing through the vessel, they were able to fight in brief, intense periods, but they only managed to delay the advance before falling back. The purpose was to defend the vessel for as long as possible, either to repel them or scatter them far enough to regroup; but they were largely unsuccessful on both fronts. Captain Ram had been caught with his pants down. All the crew positions were defending against an attack from the northeast; the pirates had approached from the opposite direction. Quickly, John called the teams back to reorg and told them to retreat and secure the Office area where he too would hole up and prepare for his next move.

At 0615, Pirates came down from the bridge, approaching through the corridor at the rear of the vessel. Six made it that far and made a bold attempt to enter the rear of the office area. Three were shot dead by defending divers; the other three hid out in the ROV Hanger. The hand full of crew in the office managed to repel the rest of the pirates, holding them off with rifle and machine gun fire. They had made a request for support, but only roughly five minutes passed before the Captain had to surrender to the pirates. If John had done an “Ammo and Casualty check” right, then he would have reported: How many rounds fired? and how many casualties? His report would contain, Total 9mm x 34, Total 5.56mm x 255, Total 7.62mm x 690, 66mm x 5, hand grenades M67 x 6. Not bad for a 20-minute fire fight, but one casualty and one injury.

Chapter 6: Pirate boarding

Every ocean wave is a pirate.

They were marched down the stairs. In single file, they then passed through the Mess room and out of the Vessel. One by one, weapons were taken from them. they were searched by a small group of Somalian pirates. There were ten of them on the back deck, no more, machine guns out, grenades hanging off their belts. They shouted at them, barking out orders, but few of us spoke any Somalian. So could hardly understand what they were saying, but clearly understood the scope of the situation. When the vessel was empty of crew, they were told to lay face down in the deck, hands up above their heads, and feet out. somewhere in the group of people preparing to deal with us, a photographer began snapping pictures. Within hours of that photographer snapping that picture, the black and white image spread around the world. This was big news.

Reported by Reuters: Satellite tracking data showed the ship appeared to have rounded the Horn of Africa and was going south past the Somali port of Hafun before suddenly turning sharply to the north and docking in Bereeda. Pictures sent to Reuters from Bereeda showed the DSV, a small Diving vessel that carries a multi-cultural crew. the governor of Gardafu in the semi-autonomous northern region of Puntland, said the ship was travelling from Qatar to Mogadishu port when pirates attacked it, in what would be the first successful hijacking since 2017.There were 60 crew onboard, said a resident in contact with the men who had seized the ship. A regional security official said the men appeared to have links to a local militia that functioned as a police unit in the Bari region. The official asked not to be named as he was not authorised to speak to the media.

Jay Bagri, a Somali piracy expert who was previously head of a United Nations group of experts enforcing an arms embargo on Somalia, said that being a pirate and a member of the Somali police had not historically been mutually exclusive. He said it appeared that a group of men wearing police uniforms had boarded the ship, robbed the crew and taken the weapons of a private security team on board. The man reported to be the ringleader of the attack on the DSV had repeated phone contact with another pirate who was part of a group that carried out Somalia's last hijacking in 2017, he added. The contact happened in the months prior to the 2017 hijacking. "If it was indeed the police, it bears resemblance to one of the earliest Somali piracy incidents, when members of the Puntland coast guard hijacked the boat they were supposed to be guarding," the semiautonomous north eastern region of Puntland, where pirates flourish. Yet control is slipping away. Driving through one of the "controlled" districts to find that its main road has been blocked off, after a policeman was shot dead there. Somalia's ongoing malaise is bewildering to outsiders. going into these war-torn countries trying not to be pessimists, but in Somalia people have to recognize that the cynics those who dismiss peace initiatives as doomed to fail—have turned out to be right for almost 20 years. Scepticism about Somalia's fragile government who hold only seven of Mogadishu's 18 districts. The latest fighting has killed more than 200 people and displaced tens of thousands more. Why is the violence so intractable? Pirates on the Indian Ocean have waylaid dozens of foreign vessels bearing food aid. Food prices were high here even before last year's worldwide spike, thanks to drought, militia roadblocks, and a devalued currency. The result is that millions now depend on food aid. The fresh fighting is pushing the country toward an unprecedented humanitarian crisis.

The European Union Naval Force, known as EU Navfor, was checking on the incident, said a source in their Somalia Joint Operation Centre. At the height of their power in 2011, Somali pirates launched 237 attacks off the coast of the country, the International Maritime Bureau says, and held hundreds hostage. The number of attacks later tumbled as shipping firms implemented better security protocols, including posting look-outs, sailing further away from Somalia, and hiring private security. International warships operating as part of a coalition also prevented several attacks Somalia has been riven by civil war since 1991 and is controlled by a patchwork of local militias, pockets of federal forces, African Union peacekeepers and Islamist insurgents. The Horn of Africa nation has also been intermittently plagued by pirates.

What the picture meant needed no interpretation. A failed set of United Nations talks had led to this, and the pirates had beaten the Diving crew. Forget about the number of pirates and the element of surprise; forget that not a single Diver died in losing. The circumstances hardly seemed to matter. The DSV had been compromised. Even though the word spread at a snail's pace compared to what it does now, it still did not take long to reach the opposing governments. The image of a dozen British Divers face down on the main deck with Somalia pirates prowling up their backs, machine guns pointed, got blood boiling throughout the world. Everything else would go on immediate hold while a response was sorted out. John is in that picture. Even more curious to think back now is that in the halls of power, someone saw him. in a prone, helpless position that would ultimately serve as a sabre-rattling call for revenge. A few of the guys look like they are craning for a look, hopeful of an opportunity to fight back. Then john remembers that he was deathly afraid of what came next. He did not speak a single word of their language. All that he can remember was the click of boot heels, the sounds of uncertain chatter and the clangs of metal against metal as their weapons piled up outside. John knew they were there by sound though and as the arrogant captors humiliated them, they are not going to kill them thought John. We are all going to make it through this, worth more alive than dead.

Chapter 7: Taken as hostages.

Hostages want to survive - they are extremely focused on their own little view of things.

Divers are used to living in confined spaces Inside the 12-man saturation complex the divers live, eat and sleep in an area less than a normal one-bedroom size. Sleeping bunks are double lined along the chamber and fold away when not used. Saturation systems usually involve more than one interconnected chamber and the 'diving bell' plus all its handling equipment. These are much more complex and usually permanently onboard the vessel. There will be a formal diving safety management system for operations, with a minimum 24-hour manned level including separate diving supervisors and life support technicians who control and manage the 'living chambers. There is a complex infrastructure of gas supplies predominantly heliox, usually with gas reclamation and recycling, given the high cost and relative rarity of this gas. Saturation systems have internal environmental control including temperature and humidity management and carbon dioxide scrubbing. It is essential that these chambers are kept spotlessly clean and that good housekeeping and personal hygiene are strictly observed to minimize all risk of infection, it is imperative that a high standard of personal hygiene is maintained within the Saturation complex. Being kept inside a few rooms by pirate guards was not really going to phase out the divers who would be accustomed to the Claustrophobia the irrational fear of confined spaces. The Life support technicians now replaced by pirates who would bring food and water. The typical system consists of temperature and humidity control, carbon dioxide removal, and equipment moni-toring. Processing consists of filtering particulate matter, removing carbon dioxide and gaseous odours, and controlling heat and humidity. The sanitary system consists of hot and cold-water supplies for operating the wash basin, shower, and toilet. Waste from the toilet discharges into a separate holding tank for proper disposal through the support platform's collection, holding, and transfer system. Pretty much like living onboard the DSV. they are not in any way spacious; they are even the mildest claustrophobe's worst nightmare. John entering that first hatch puts him in a miniscule round room known as the "wet pot." It is used to transfer the divers to the diving bell through a hatch in the ceiling—and it is also the bathroom, with a tiny metal sink, toilet, and showerhead. Through the wet pot, another hatch leads to the living space, where there is just enough room for four to six seats around a removable aluminium table. In other words, for up to six weeks, the divers will spend their waking hours either under hundreds of feet of water on the ocean floor or squeezed into an area the size of a small bathroom. Beyond that, past a droopy blue curtain, is the sleeping area, with six double-stacked bunks squeezed into a "U" shape. The bunks at the far end are partially blocked by the others, and therefore particularly cramped So bunk choice is a big deal. In the divers draw lots, or whoever gets there first. But at least divers do all get their own sleeping spaces. In the bad old days, John Remembers six guys would have to hot-bed three bunks, with one group working while the other slept. There are still ways to keep the work going 24/7. On some vessels, up to four saturation chambers can be linked together through side hatches in the wet pots and connected by large metal hamster tubes. This enables multiple dive teams to be in constant rotation. Once the divers are tightly ensconced in the saturation chamber, the life support crew begins pumping in heliox, and the "blowdown" begins. During the blowdown, the rapid increase in atmospheric pressure makes the chamber ridiculously hot and humid. John and his team felt like they were in "Blowdown" right now as the building had no Air conditioning, and the temperature was nearly unbearable.

The notion of becoming a "Hostage" arrives with a dubious sense. They have all seen the movies. They have internalized images of ragged men shivering in a bitter cold, beaten, and taunted and sorely underfed by their captors. Everyone has seen and pondered over this dilemma as well. It is a far better fate to die with your boots on than to linger helplessly as a captive. All the lads on the team were past that fear for their lives but were not far enough into the clear to be comfortable. A hundred thoughts raced through john's head like loose threads unravelling all at once. Most of them fell under some category of, what is going on? Quite several decades had passed since the British government had encountered the dilemma of having hostages - what to do and how to negotiate their release. Marine training does not tell you precisely what to do when taken hostage, but the implication should be clear. Maintain a strong stance, put up a wall of defiance. Do not say a word. Do not give the enemy anything to use against them, cool bravado in their eyes, and a ready posture. What? The pirates are not getting anything out of them.

After they were all sorted and ordered like heads of cattle, the lads in the dive team were escorted by a small group of pirates, the same pirates they fired on throughout the morning. The hour was dragging on toward the afternoon, and the panic of what would happen to the divers as newly captured prisoners was wearing thinner with each moment. Although these underfed bastards were strutting around and posing for celebratory pictures, they were as scared as we were - probably more so. They're not going to line us up and shoot us, John thought. We are not going to be humiliated or made an example of; that had already happened in the moment that we threw our hands up. By now, the news had been broadcast to the world. The worst was over with. What would be coming next, however, remained curiously up in the air. An eerie calm came spread over them as they lined up in an orderly fashion and sat down quietly on the deck. not one of the Divers had much to say. All the faces were there, Johno and Alex and Pete. We exchanged a few sideways glances, darting eyes between familiar faces. What we managed to convey in that silence was a well-heeled sense of scepticisms at best. We sat around for quite a long time while the Somali pirates waited on their orders. As they watched them operate, John realized that they were worried. Perhaps they had not expected to succeed as they had? Finally, the vessel engine started.

One of the Somali Pirates piped up, bravely breaking the icy silence. "Do you think you'll be back here?" he asked. John bristled at the sound of his voice, his words of broken English. Every one of the Divers would have answered him similarly had they drummed up enough nerve to speak their minds in that moment. Only one of them did though. "Sure, we will be back," one Diver replied.

Had that bold Diver given the Pirates anything by vocalizing defiance? Could he take that back to his commander and use it against them? Who knows? All that John can say, looking at that moment, is that it felt good to hear the diver say that he would be back. A lot can change in a short time. Although the rest of the ride out, only took a few moments, a critical shift had occurred. They felt as though they were already gaining back the upper hand on these guys, who so wrongly believed that the divers would all simply give in. That Pirate needed to be aware. He needed a lesson in the simple fact that the Divers does not whimper when stricken; he roars. ordered off the vessel. A deafening wind confronted them as, once again, they were lined up and sorted out. A fast boat awaited, and they boarded, like schoolchildren on a trip, in single file. they had already been ordered to surrender their weapons. Now lined up and awaiting orders to get on the FRC, they were given a full body search. John remembers one of the lads had a six-inch knife hidden in his boot. When the Somali pirate found it and held out the steel blade, the lads all got a surprisingly good laugh. The look on the pirates faces though. Pure panic. What was that Divers' intent? Was he going to run every pirate through while on the FRC? On board, we looked around the boat as we took seats. Although uncomfortable, a comforting sense of familiarity came over me. The divers were being combined with a few lads from Marine crew the smoke had hardly been extinguished, but DSV Team was already reforming. John heard the Fast craft propellers sputter to a start. he took a deep breath as he backed slowly up along the DSV, held for a moment, and then sped out toward the dusk grey horizon, now reduced to a jagged outline. John craned my head to watch, as everything behind got smaller and eventually disappeared. They were on their journey, the DSV growing smaller with each second.

The boat ride took them on a southwest route across the Indian Ocean. Similar understandings dawned on each of them: everything seemed to be fine, aside from our giving up, which was feeling more and more like a small diversion. As we flattened out at cruising speed, a bit of laughter played amongst a few of the lads. The divers cracked jokes. A few of the guys had been brimming with stories, boasting loudly about what had happened during the morning firefight. The way John saw it, there was no use in missing out on all the fun. he told the story of shooting through the port hole glass with his gun. The tale got a few nods from the lads and more than a few laughs. Those questions of how he would respond under fire were a thing of the past. What had started out that morning as an uncertainty had been solidified on that boat ride. Survivor of a firefight, I was not only a Diver. he had become a Diving Superintendent.

Under a pitch-black sky, the fast boat began a gradually slow down. As they looked out to see that they were approaching a small town with a smattering of surface lights. The boat touched the quay side at Somali town, a base in southern Somalia. Once on the ground, a team of pirates surrounded them. Their guns were pointed as the divers were shuffled between vehicles, this time to a bus. Although no one knew where, at least they were driving off over land. At the front of the bus, John and Johno took their seats. They eventually reached a town in Somalia. Only a few days before, the DSV had been on its way to Oman for dry-docking - now that seemed like a lifetime ago. Unlike at the last place, there was no pirates, with their guns trained on them. they were transported by a normal bus john was scared shitless, but a sense of scepticism had crept in and taken over. Where were we being taken? A camp? A prison? The only unfamiliar face aboard that bus was the driver, who steered us through the night. John nodded off a few times, only to startle and look out, unable to see more than the roadside around him. Only a short distance down the highway, the lights of civilization reappeared on the horizon., lounging on bullet-pocked street corners and spaced out in the back of pickup trucks, Kalashnikovs in their hands and nowhere to go. To them, law and order are thoroughly abstract concepts. To them, the only law in the land is the business end of a machine gun. Everyone craned eagerly as what appeared to be a hotel emerged ahead. The bus pulled off the highway into an empty parking lot, where the pirate vehicles lined up and stopped. The pirates got out and prepared to move us. Everyone shot a look around, wondering what was going on. This cannot really be happening, can it? What are we doing at a hotel? they were escorted off the transports and into the evening air. The lack of a bitter, stiff wind in the face felt good. Despite uncertainty, the air was refreshing. Despite the unfamiliarity with the place, they sure knew what they looked like when we saw them. The hotel we had been brought to be a four-star affair. John can still recall the outline of dim moonlight on the beach, spread as far in either direction as his eye could see. The view was unforgettable. It was the kind of thing that a, Notts born lad can only dream of until he sees it for himself.

Locals in Puntland note that the millions of ransom dollars have resulted in the creation of secondary businesses in the region. Negotiations require radio and cell phone communication and technology. Feeding hostages requires restaurants and shops with western foods. The pirates' consumer interests require salesmen and mechanics. Building beachfront mansions requires carpenters, and suppliers. Financing of pirate operations require venture capitalists, many of them local people.

There are many repercussions when a hostage-taking incident takes place, even if it reaches a successful conclusion. Regardless of outcome, there undoubtedly is residual trauma to the victims—if not physical, certainly emotional, and mental. The hostage-taker is taking chances with his own life because impaired judgment or the wrong decision overall could result in his own death. Consequently, it is essential to have a well-trained negotiator, carefully attuned to the "curves" encountered when dealing with a hostage-taker. Add to the explosive nature of a hostage taking incident by having it occur in a foreign country, and the risks are seriously multiplied. It is a volatile environment at best. The Pirates often have a "What do we have to lose?" mentality and need little excuse to act out. One of the most interesting dimensions of a hostage-taking incident occurring is the fact that the hostage takers are often knowledgeable about the environment and routine. it is not like an incident that has erupted in an unfamiliar locale. This makes the element of surprise less effective, as the hostage-taker will be more edgy and reactive to any unexpected movement or event. There is little room for error or for heated exchanges.

Chapter 8: Training

It's a state of mind.

The Royal Marines are the UK's elite amphibious force, going where others will not and doing things others cannot. First on the scene where needed, anywhere in the world. It is a state of mind. experts in getting the job done, whatever the conditions. Against the odds. In tropical heat and extreme cold. Whether there is a need for speed, or a need for stamina. Because all highly skilled commandos who have been through some of the most rigorous training on the planet. defined by history, heritage is important. because the operations tackled, and the battles won have helped shape the world-famous state of mind. Striving for excellence and adapting to an ever-changing world is what defines the modern Royal Marine from the skills gained and the role they play, to the values they demonstrate. Earning the green beret and embarking on some of the British military's toughest operations takes a unique set of personal qualities and skills. Royal Marines Commandos are the ultimate soldier, developing through an unflinching commitment. Each Commando spends two years as a General Duties Marine, learning the essential skills needed to become an elite amphibious soldier. After that, starting as a specialist in anything from mortars to signals. Over the course of his career, John will complete multiple training courses, constantly expanding his skillset.

Life in the Royal Marines is unique. There is a bond between Commandos which comes from living, working, and socialising together. Supporting each other is at the heart of their ethos and is why they can be the first to understand, the first to adapt and respond, and the first to overcome. Many of the attributes required to be successful are the same as those required on the battlefield, from the physical and mental strength it takes to win, to the all-important determination and teamwork. That is why each

Commando is actively encouraged to pursue outside interests and is supported with training facilities and time off to train. It is not just the extreme weather that makes operating in the middle east so challenging. It's the harsh and unforgiving nature of the sea. That is why training onboard the DSV is so vital, because they can adapt to handle those brutal conditions, they can handle anything. John among the most skilled at desert warfare. Whether combatting hostile forces, training crew, or deploying on a diving operation, they have the skills and experience to get the job done. unique state of mind is put to the test in aa offshore environment. It is where they blend in, patiently waiting for the right moment, whatever the operation. As soon as they get onboard, it becomes habitat, where they do not just survive; they thrive.

The work of former Royal Marines is hidden from the public eye. on operations, at high readiness to deploy for operations. flexibility enables them to undertake numerous roles from conflict prevention to specialist amphibious operations. It's a great working environment onboard, enjoyable and challenging with a sense of belonging to something very special.to become one of the world's most elite amphibious force and wear the coveted green beret. Digging deep to aim high, stop for nothing. In the most hostile environments, and on the most treacherous seas. no such thing as an average day on the DSV, and there is no such thing as an average guy. They need to be exceptional just like the rest of the team, and the same state of mind. Play a key role in dealing with occurring crises. Missions will be varied, ranging from amphibious pirates, to combat operations. Developing his military skills, before selecting a specialisation to become what he was today. Traveling the world, protecting the interests as part of a team renowned for its unity and brotherhood. With special bonds with diver mates that will never be broken.

Essential military skills, specialisation such as abseiling, assault engineering, combat intelligence. Tough. That is what being a Royal Marine is, and what they need to earn your green beret in the first place. There is a reason they are the most elite amphibious troops in the world. It is because they stop for nothing. A huge part of life is the brotherhood. This is teamwork like no one has ever experienced before. the opportunity to push training every day, experiencing a lifestyle never imagined. One where doing vital work every day, all over the world. The challenges faced, immense, but so are the rewards.

There is a natural sorting out that takes place in the military. It is not a very subtle process, but the pecking order must be established. As a Marine, if you made it through basic training, odds are, they were the toughest guy from their school or town. The lad next to him was the toughest guy in his school too, and so was the guy next to him, and so on and so on. In a unit full of tough necks, where everyone was a brash alpha male, the process of sorting out often lacks all the elements of nuance.

Everyone strutted around the barracks, or while out on leave, with a whole hell of a lot to prove. Who they had to prove themselves to was entirely up to them There was not a single Royal Marine among them who was accustomed to taking a step down, so whenever provoked or otherwise tested, they had no choice but to prove to the guy whose fists were raised, and lips curled hatefully that you belonged in the ring with him?

Proving yourself came down in one of two ways, fighting being first. The other way was drinking. A Marine had to be proficient in either one. Odds were, however, that the two ways went hand in hand. John spent a countless lot of those early days in uniform, fighting and drinking his way through life. When the dust settled, the Marines had to prove themselves worthy in another pursuit, which they called “trapping.” They were relentless in trying to score with the Girls. Everywhere he went was a process of talking tough, drinking a lot of whatever he could get our hands on, and then finding someone to trap. John’s appetite for women was voracious. he chased them like medals. he was relentless from the moment he was enlisted in the Commandos. In a lot of ways, looking back on those rough, early days, He can see now that everyone went through life with blinkers on. Maybe John knew this much going in, and maybe I did not. Either way, the path to surviving his time in the Marines was clear. he would have to fight his way through. He had taken beatings, more than his share. Often, though, John doled out a good account too. John was not afraid of proving himself that’s what it boiled down to. He was not an ambitious type of recruit. As he came into his own as a Marine and a man, he did not have sights set on moving up. Unlike some of the others, he was not bent on becoming a higher rank. John wanted to survive.

Training was rough, no doubt about it. Marines are a tough lot that do a lot of hard drinking. John proved to be no different. Every night, him and his mates drank until they were pissed. Often, did not return until one of them had been in a bar or street brawl. Every weekend or leave, they went out drinking and trapping. To say they were reckless may be right. Most of what mattered was how hard they fought and how well they trapped. They were a large part of gaining respect. A military life breeds toughness. Marines are hardened through training, as well as while they are away from camp. No one could back down from a fight, it simply was not how that was done. Whether or not the girl was a beauty, to turn her down was unconscionable. Survival and advancement of respect are relentless pursuits. Being combat green was difficult on a Marine. John’s unit was split almost perfectly in two, the guys who had seen combat and those who had not. A few guys in his unit were recently returned from deployment. Some had been to Northern Ireland, fighting the IRA street to street, house to house in some of the most complicated guerrilla and terrorist fighting in British military history. Others had been further away, fighting in campaigns in Asia, Europe, and Africa. A few were decorated and could boast of medals and a haughty stream of recognition. Wherever they went, the experienced guys commanded immediate respect. No matter how hard they fought, or well they trapped, what kind of Marine you would be in a firefight could only be proven one way. No one pined for warfare, but quietly, they all welcomed the opportunity to act.

Chapter 9: First Taste of Combat

"I could get killed out here"?

Look down the valley! See the cloud that overshadows it! I tell you that the cloud of murder hangs thicker and lower than that over the heads of the people. It is the Valley of Fear, the Valley of Death. The terror is in the hearts of the people from the dusk to the dawn. he who lives by the gun dies by the gun those people who commit violent acts must expect to suffer violence themselves.

Just nineteen years old when John had his first taste of combat. looking back on those events and recalling how everything played out over those manic two and a half months in the Falklands, a great deal of those details come across as blurry. Some of the names and faces are hard to arrive at, even when he sits down quietly and grasp around in his mind for them. Some things, however, a man simply does not forget. Perhaps it is that he cannot. Every single one of us has something, maybe even a few moments from their past, that they simply cannot bring themselves to let go of. a great many of those moments took place back in 1982. John had recently enlisted in the Royal Marine Commandos.

He earned a Green Beret. When you reach that level, it means you are part of something special. I was part of a small detachment to be stationed on the Falkland Islands for one year called NP8901. Maybe he had indeed heard of the Falkland Islands before choosing to go there, but do not recall. Either way, they meant nothing special to me. The other Marines and John had been on the islands a day, at our barracks, in an area called Moody Brook, there is not a lot out there just a main road. Directly to the east, the boggy grass gave way to a body of water. We did not know our way around. The largest town or settlement was called Stanley, by late in March, though, they had all been made aware that at least some fighting was imminent. There was tension in the air. Aggressive overtures by the Argentine army revealed that they stood on the brink of invasion, ready to take back the islands that they thought were rightfully theirs. It was around 3 P.M. Local time, on the previous day, when the other shoe finally dropped on us. It was on a Thursday, April 1 when Rex Hunt, British Governor of the Falkland Islands, received an ominous telex from British Intelligence. "We have apparently reliable evidence that an Argentine task force will gather off Cape Pembroke early tomorrow morning, 2nd April. You will wish to make your dispositions accordingly." John was still a fresh face beneath his Green Beret. He had yet to engage in any combat during his short Marine career but knew what the intelligence call meant. Making our dispositions was a military euphemism for "Get the boys ready to fight." Every one of us made the same translation. This was not the first message either. Days earlier, an intercepted message to the Argentine submarine Santa Fe revealed that a few of the South American reconnaissance troops would be landing on the beach at Mullet Creek, roughly fifteen kilometres down the road from where we stood. Later, our detachment sorted out the news while hanging around in the bar located in our barracks. As john remember, the boys from NP8901 were there, along with twenty Royal Navy personnel. Everyone rapt with attention, listening as Boss Major Mike Norman pepped them up with a forceful plan of action. The Major was a strident man. And they had already seen that he was given to stormy fits of bluster. His words as he paced back and forth came across as urgent and forceful. To anyone who was listening, what came next was as clear as a bell. "Today you are going to die," he roared ominously at the sea of blank faces staring back in his direction. "So, go out there and do the job you were trained to do." My heart sank a little bit. I was not ready to die. As I glanced sideways over at the chap next to me, a Royal Navy medic whose face was already as pale as a ghost, john realized that he felt the same way. he was only nineteen years old. Could this really be the end? There was nothing to be done, though, no protest. The order had been given. Now it was time to act. A mixed mood took hold of the room. A sombre air captivated some of the faces, while others were aroused, seemingly ready to relish the coming fight. As Norman finished his rallying of the boys, the meeting broke up and everyone fell in line. grabbing his kit and machine gun. One of his mates, Gaz, quipped as they hurried to join their section. "No point in getting your head down now," he said. Gaz was right. This is a story, but as it turns out, it is there in the history books too. John was one of those frightened lads in that dingy bar at Moody Brook barracks. Like now they were the last and only line of defence. All that stood between the Falkland Islands, a British territory for more than a century, was in their ability to repel an uncertain army of invaders.

hostage rescue attempts which have failed. The Iran hostage rescue attempt is one of the greatest military misfortunes of modern warfare, specifically in the hostage rescue arena. It is a perfect example of how highly skilled and trained personnel, placed in an uncertain environment, fail at what they are supposed to do best. Throughout history, counterterrorist forces have been sent into high-risk situations in uncertain environments and have often failed in the face of uncertainty, a mob of Iranian Islamic militants, using a crowd of student protesters as a deception screen, overran the American Embassy in downtown Teheran. More than 100 people were taken hostage, including many Americans, after five months of tense negotiations to release the American hostages had failed, President Jimmy Carter sent a military rescue mission into Iran, composed of Army, Navy, Air Force and Marines, to rescue the American hostages. The rescue mission was aborted after three RH-53D helicopters broke down in route to Dasht-e-Kavir, the remote desert site known as DESERT ONE. During exfiltration procedures from DESERT ONE, two aircraft collided while attempting to reposition during refuelling; eight crewmembers, five from the U.S. Air Force and three U.S. Marines, died because of the engulfing fires from the crash. The mission was a complete failure, and even though a new rescue plan was developed, no other rescue attempts were made to free the hostages. Recce troop with a combat controller from the Air Force to recce the landing strip at DESERT ONE and place landing lights, and another troop to recce the actual grounds in Tehran and prepare a welcoming committee with vehicles. Both operations were highly dangerous and proved to be successful, but the intelligence collected during these operations was not disseminated.

The weather conditions were critical in adding uncertainty during the operation, specifically for the pilots, increasing the difficulty of flying under such conditions. The uncertainty of the condition in which the hostages were in as well as an increasingly hostile attitude by the government of Iran, added to the volatility of the environment, thus precipitating the President's decision to act. No one really knew the condition of the hostages. The lack of contingency rehearsals added uncertainty during the infiltration phase. The inexperience of the Marine pilots being placed in an uncertain environment that was inevitably hostile, and expected to conduct a high-risk, high skill level task with little or no preparation, was a recipe for failure.

Surprise, the element of surprise was never considered as a principle to provide leverage and achieve operational superiority over the enemy. Throughout all phases of the planned operation, there was an ever-present feeling of wishful thinking, hoping that each stage of the phased infiltration would work and that none of the elements would be compromised. Surprise was lost as soon as the rescue elements landed on DESERT ONE. Immediately upon arrival, the Marine security element had to open fire on a passenger bus, creating large fires and explosions in the middle of the desert; surprise was impossible to recover after that one incident. In addition, a vehicle infiltration into the target area, in the middle of Tehran, is considered an emergency deliberate assault. Even if everything had gone as planned, the element of surprise would have been lost immediately preventing the assault force to take any advantage of it.

One of the biggest failures was the inability to match the technical systems to the operator's skills. General Vaught misused the robust communications package due to the restrictions and the inordinate control of mission execution. The new systems for the helicopters and the lack of experience of the Marine pilots caused great uncertainty, especially flying with night vision devices pilots complained of vertigo and could not see each other through the dust clouds. They failed to anticipate the proper number of aircraft required to conduct the operation by not taking into consideration the failure rates for the helicopter force. A force of 8 helicopters was launched on mission day from the USS Nimitz, in hopes of having 6 helicopters arrive at the target site. By doing a simple probabilistic analysis for the helicopter force, using helicopter data and actual success ratios, can be calculated that to have 6 operational helicopters at the target site they should have sent at least 10 helicopters. also failed to anticipate changes in the environment by not having contingency plans to respond to the changing weather and aircraft mishaps. A fatal error for the rescue operation was that no full-dress rehearsals took place. Disparate groups of different units cobbled together in haste attempted to synchronize their work literally on the fly the very last rehearsal conducted by anyone in the raiding force had taken place three weeks prior to the operation. Each element conducted its own rehearsal, but the force never got together as a whole. It was assumed that everyone would do his job and get to DESERT ONE and to the objective on his own. Many changes were made during the last three weeks prior to the operation, especially with the air movement. The communications plan between elements was completely flawed; the operators and the C-130's were the only elements with secure communications capability. To make matters worse, there was no bump plan in place in case of aircraft failure. The very nature of a hostage rescue operation is a highly technical and complex endeavour. It takes specially selected and well-trained individuals who are self-reliant and can operate well under pressure. Special Operators cannot be mass-produced overnight. it is a long process of training and dedication to reach the level of professionalism required by personnel. Delta Force had been activated only a few hours prior to the hostage situation. Colonel Beckwith was alerted to the hostage situation on his way back from Delta's culmination and capabilities exercise. This operation would be their validation and the opportunity for Colonel Beckwith to show off his new force. Each component of the force conducted a series of rehearsals throughout the planning phases of the operation. Delta Force conducted over 90 rehearsals. Overall, there were only seven combined rehearsals, each involving only a few of the components from the rescue force. The members of the newly formed Delta Force had just been officially certified and had tremendous pressure to excel and prove themselves as the world's number one counter terrorist force. On the other hand, the helicopter crews lacked the internal drive and pressure to excel. The pilots and crews did not waste any time when it came time to abort the operation. They failed to adapt to a complex environment and continue with the operation. The pilots for the helicopter force received highly specialized training. Flying at night with NVDs still was considered a dangerous operation, one rarely done by any aviator. Pilots had to train extensively flying with NVDs. The initial group of helicopter pilots had come from the Navy; after several rehearsals, the whole group was disbanded due to their inability to fly at night. Col Beckwith and Col Kyle later would recruit Marine pilots to replace the Navy pilots. Some would argue that the Marine pilots were given the mission only to have representatives from each service. The Marine pilots had to go through a train up phase to become familiar with the new technology as well as with new helicopters. RH-53D minesweeper helicopters were reconfigured and outfitted with fuel blivits for the extended flight to Tehran. Marine pilots had to get used to flying these aircraft for extended periods, while under strict radio silence, limiting their ability to check with one another. The planners overestimated the ability of the helicopter pilots in accomplishing the mission. The pilots had trained together as a group for a period of only five months with new equipment and helicopters, and it was assumed that this training would be enough.

The deception plan for the operation was non-existent. Deception was only seen as a means of survivability, by camouflaging helicopters and utilizing minesweeper equipment to eliminate their signature. The only resemblance of any deception plan was used by the advance party elements already in country, pre-staging the vehicles to be used by the assault force. Their deception plan was based on survivability and not linked to a surprise attack. With advance reconnaissance elements already operating around the target area, it would have been a perfect opportunity to devise a distraction or some sort of a ruse to aid in the covering the assault force's infiltration. Deception allows operational leverage for the assault force, and it gives them the opportunity to surprise the enemy, based on accurate intelligence. None of these factors were at play during the operation.

At the conclusion of Operation and towards the end, to examine what went wrong with the operation and make improvements and recommendations to prevent another disaster of this magnitude. Twenty-three issues were identified and investigated because of the operation, and eleven of these were categorized as having a direct impact on the outcome of the operation. Colonel James H. Kyle lists four of these findings as critical in the failure of the operation. First, alternate helicopter pilots should have been selected to team with Marines. Second, helicopter aborts—pilots lacked certain knowledge vital to reaching an informed decision whether to abort or to proceed. Third, enemy radar threat—helicopter pilots based low-level tactics on erroneous intelligence reports. Fourth, helicopter communications, pilots lacked secure modes of communication to receive vital mission information. In the end, the Holloway Commission determined that the overriding cause for the mission abort was an unexpected helicopter failure rate and low-visibility flight conditions en route to Desert One While overconfidence in one's abilities seems to be one of the most overwhelming common denominators in most of SF failures, in the case of DESERT ONE it was the lack of confidence of the helicopter pilots that caused the decision to abort. The inexperience of the Marine pilots flying the helicopters, the mechanical failures of the helicopters, and the reluctance of the pilots to continue and complete the mission, were the root problems of why the operation was called off. Colonel Beckwith did not exhibit overconfidence when it came time to stick to his abort criteria of no less than six helicopters, based on labour and the tasks to be accomplished by his operators. In the end the mission could have been completed if the helicopter pilots had had the guts to try.

The operation never made it past DESERT ONE. All remaining personnel were transloaded into the remaining C-141 aircrafts to return to their home stations, without ever attempting a follow up rescue. Planning for a second rescue continued for the remaining part of the year, but no follow-on rescue was ever attempted. Eventually, all hostages were released minutes after President Reagan was inaugurated into office in 1980. The total duration for the hostage siege was 444 days.

Operation Nimrod on the other hand was “text” book Six Iranian Arabs from Khuzestan attacked the Iranian Embassy in London, which was located at 16 Princes Gate, and took the people in the embassy hostage. The hostages were chiefly Iranian embassy staff but also included several tourists and two BBC personnel who were in the embassy to pick up visas. The total number of hostages was 26 the group identified themselves as members of the Democratic Revolutionary Front for the Liberation of Arabistan, which sought independence for the oil-rich southwestern region of Iran, Khuzestan. The leader of the hostage takers was Oan, codenamed Salim. His demands were autonomy for “Arabistan” the release of 91 Arabian detainees from Iranian prisons, and safe passage for them. The hostage takers declared the deadline as noon on Thursday, May 1. If their demands not met, they would blow up the embassy with the hostages inside. As soon as the British government had become aware of the incident, the Metropolitan Police and cordoned off the area. The police were not the only force involved; the SAS was aware of the crisis from the beginning. The commander of the 22 SAS, Lieutenant Colonel Mike Rose, ordered his team to be on 24-hour standby to conduct a hostage rescue operation after receiving a call from a former SAS soldier who was working with the Metropolitan Office. Afterward, Colonel Rose tried to get confirmation from his headquarters; then, the SAS headquarters asked to obtain confirmation from the Ministry of Defence. When competent authorities failed to respond to his question with a definitive answer, he decided to go to London to conduct a preliminary reconnaissance before receiving an official order from the headquarters. The official order came six hours later from the Minister of Defence when Colonel Rose was already on the scene. Prime Minister Margaret Thatcher preferred not to directly intervene in the management of the crisis and delegated that authority to the "Home Secretary,"

William Whitelaw. With the police securing the area, Whitelaw gathered a crisis management team consisting of senior members of the Home Office. the Ministry of Defence, the Foreign Office, the Metropolitan Police, MI6, MI5, a representative of SAS—de la Billiere—and the public utilities including the gas board, the water board, and the British Airports Authority in the Cabinet Office Briefing Room (COBRA).

The COBRA served as the British government's emergency committee to observe and administer the efforts to solve the evolving crisis. As a leader of the COBRA, Whitelaw was never autocratic; he always let people express their ideas and concerns. Before every critical decision, he brought the problem into a discussion without leaving anything in the air. During the crisis, Whitelaw kept in contact with the prime minister. Thatcher and Whitelaw were on the same page about the strategy that included four criteria. First, the police would continue the negotiations to end the crisis peacefully. Second, if hostage takers shot anybody without even killing him or her, the military rescue option considered. Third, the SAS would get the green light to go in only if the hostage takers killed anybody. Fourth, under no circumstances would the negotiators promise to let the hostage takers out of England as free people.

Even though Thatcher was not present in the COBRA, she laid down three principles to guide the COBRA. First, the United Kingdom's laws applied to the crisis even though the hostage-taking event was in a foreign embassy. Second, under no circumstances, would hostage takers, be allowed to leave the country as free agents. Last, the priority would be a peaceful solution. Thatcher's priority was not risk hostages' lives, but at the same time, she wanted to show the international community that terrorism should be defeated.

The Iranian government's reaction to the crisis made the situation more complicated. The Iranian foreign minister acknowledged to British decision makers that Iran would not meet any of the terrorists' demands. Furthermore, Iran announced that if terrorists killed any of the hostages, the same number of Iranian Arabs, executed. The foreign minister also accused the United States and the Central Intelligence Agency (CIA) of being behind the incident. The Iranian government's attitude put all responsibilities on the British authorities. After reaching the scene, the 22 SAS Task Force members settled into a building close to the Iranian Embassy and immediately planned for an emergency rescue. To reduce the risk, the SAS team needed more time and intelligence. The intelligence service was trying to get intelligence about the building, hostage takers, and even the hostages. In this respect, the intelligence service gathered important information about the interior of the building from the people who recently visited the embassy and from the first released hostage. In addition, the planners wanted real-time intelligence from the inside of the building. Thus, the intelligence service decided to place listening devices on walls adjacent to the embassy. The walls were too thick for planting those devices, so the agents had to thin the walls. The noise of the thinning work would need covered by something loud. The decision makers in the COBRA coordinated with airport authorities to make several airplanes fly at low altitudes to cover the noise of the preparations to install the listening devices. In the meantime, the negotiation process continued to try to end the crisis peacefully while gaining time for the planners and the intelligence gathering efforts. In the meantime, the first deadline passed without any problems. Salim, the leader of the hostage takers, released many women hostages and a BBC member who had a severe stomach condition. However, the situation inside the Iranian Embassy was getting worse day by day. In addition to the previous demands, Salim wanted three ambassadors from any Arab countries to act as negotiators to be able to get out of the country with his men by plane. The British decision makers did not feel comfortable with the idea of foreign diplomat mediators. The decision makers' major concern was how to control the situation if forced to use negotiators whom they could not trust. Furthermore, the new demand was not consistent with one of Thatcher's principles: do not let the terrorist's escape. The next day, May 2, Salim wanted to make an announcement on the BCC and wanted a reporter to come and take this statement. He also insisted that the announcement aired exactly as he wrote it. However, the BBC did not make the announcement, as he wanted; they misrepresented his announcement and did not mention that the hostage takers wanted the Arab diplomats in England to negotiate with the British Government. Thus, the tension in the hostage situation rose.

The reluctance of the British decision makers to consider working with Arab negotiators slowed the process of contacting Arab countries' embassies. Now, the attitude of the British decision makers and the inaccurate statement of the BBC made Salim furious. Salim threatened to kill a hostage unless the BBC corrected its announcement by 2100 hours. The decision makers let the BBC correct the previous announcement to ease the tension. The announcement made as the hostage takers had demanded. Thus, the hostage takers released another hostage.

In the next two days, May 4 and 5, negotiations with the hostage takers continued, but the British Government did not make any promise to them and did not bring any Arab negotiators, as the hostage takers had demanded. The COBRA did not respond to the consistent messages from police negotiators about the demand for an Arab negotiator. This problem almost brought negotiations to a standstill. Additionally, the strange noises around the embassy building and, in its walls, made the hostage takers think the police were planning a rescue operation. Therefore, the tension in the embassy increased again when the hostage takers threatened for the second time to kill hostages if their demands not met in 45 minutes. Then, three shots heard. The negotiators could not be sure about what happened. De la Billiere, the director of SAS, reported the shots to the COBRA to get permission to begin military operation. However, the Home Secretary was not present. After the call, the Home Secretary immediately came to London to discuss the military operation. In the COBRA, Home Secretary Whitelaw and the other members of the crisis management team examined all details of the military plan. De la Billiere summarized the military option and rehearsals that the SAS teams had done. At the end, Whitelaw approved the plan by telling de la Billiere that he would not interfere; and if the military operation failed, he would take full responsibility. Then, de la Billiere ordered the SAS teams to be ready to take their positions and conduct a rescue operation on short notice. The SAS teams were ready to assault with ten minutes notice. The negotiators made their last attempt to ease the tension inside the embassy by bringing an imam to talk to the leader of the hostage takers. However, Salim refused to talk with the imam; three more shots heard from the embassy. After some time, a dead body thrown outside from the main entrance of the embassy building. When medical personnel examined the body, they realized that the hostage had been dead for hours. Now, the British decision makers were sure at least one hostage killed. Whitelaw immediately contacted Thatcher to get her final approval. Thatcher approved the military rescue operation, and afterward, Whitelaw ordered de la Billiere to begin the operation; de la Billiere authorized the tactical commander, Colonel Rose, to conduct the operation.

While the SAS teams were positioning, the negotiators kept the leader of the hostage takers busy by continuing to talk with him to preserve the secrecy and create surprise during the operation. The best-trained military unit in the British Armed Forces, the SAS, was ready to rescue the hostages and eliminate the hostage takers. Operation Nimrod is one of the most famous hostage rescue operations in history.

The operation was successful because the hostages rescued with only a few casualties while neutralizing all the hostage takers. The task force for the operation consisted of two SAS teams the Red Team and the Blue Team. All SAS soldiers, highly trained professionals. The operation began at 19:23 hours on May 5. The Red team was going to rappel from the roof of the building; simultaneously the Blue team was going to enter the building from the ground floor. The simultaneous entry not achieved, because of a pre-mature initiation. Even though the uncoordinated entrance warned the hostage takers, the SAS teams stormed the building by entering from two directions evacuating the hostages. During the assault, the hostage takers had killed one of the hostages and wounded two. The operation lasted 17 minutes.

During the operation, the senior decision makers in the COBRA monitored radio communications between the SAS teams. They did not intervene in the execution phase of the operation. After the operation, Whitelaw went to the scene to thank the SAS teams as they prepared to return to base. Prime Minister Thatcher visited the base of the SAS to congratulate the SAS soldiers who executed the rescue operation. She praised their bravery and professionalism and thanked them one by one.

The British decision makers sent a clear message to the international community with Operation Nimrod that the British authorities do not make deals with terrorists and that any kind of terror actions inside Britain would not succeed. Additionally, the SAS's success demonstrated SAS professionalism to the countries considering creating their own special units to combat terrorism.

The initial plan for the rescue operation was not perfect. As time progressed, the planners improved the plan based on available intelligence. The British decision makers approved the plan only after the terrorists killed the two hostages. It is hard to understand why the British decision makers waited until the hostage takers had killed two people. They could have initiated the rescue after being sure that the operation's risk was reasonable. Additionally, the British decision makers were aware that there was no possibility of meeting the demands of the hostage takers and that negotiations would not end with a peaceful solution. Therefore, continuing the negotiations until the killings was unnecessary, especially considering they had a rescue plan with acceptable risk.

The preparation phase, the British decision makers chose the best unit in the British Armed Forces, the SAS. The rescue task force consisted of the best-trained soldiers; specially trained for counterterrorism operations. The SAS's professionalism, detailed planning, and bravery of the teams produced success. Second, the decision makers initially approved negotiations to solve the problem peacefully. However, the demands of the hostage takers were contrary to the policies that the Prime Minister and other senior decision makers agreed. This fact reduced the chance of successful negotiations and led the decision makers to think more seriously about the military rescue. Thus, after the announcement of the demands, the role of the negotiations became an effort to gain time for the military operation and convince the hostage takers to release as many hostages as possible. Although negotiations gained some time for the planners and the intelligence service, two hostages died during the negotiation process. Third, during the crisis, the British decision makers displayed good coordination. The operation benefited from the coordinated work of the COBRA. The members of the COBRA responded quickly to the needs of the SAS. For instance, in the preparation phase of the operation, the military planners needed exact intelligence to improve their plan and lessen the risk of the operation. The intelligence service, MI5, responded quickly to the demand of the military planners and planted listening devices on the walls between the Iranian Embassy and the Ethiopian Embassy. The responsive coordination of the COBRA solved the problem. The airport authorities changed the route for landing planes, which covered the noise of the thinning of the walls. In normal times, this would take days because of bureaucratic procedures. The decision to establish COBRA made the coordination easy and responsive. The British decision makers were good at coordinating among themselves. The British decision makers could not display the same coordination ability while contacting Arab diplomats to convince them to be negotiators. The British decision makers preferred to go slow. Thatcher might have accelerated the process, but she decided to delegate her authority to the Home Secretary. Because of the slow process to find Arab diplomats, the hostage-takers became angry and killed a hostage. Conceivably, if the British decision makers gave the impression of making every effort to convince Arabian diplomats to be negotiators, this may have kept the hostage takers calm, preserved the secrecy of the rescue attempt, and gained more time for the planners.

Senior civilian and military decision makers' intervention during the execution of the operation was minimal. They monitored radio communications between the SAS teams during the execution without intervening. Colonel Rose, the tactical commander, oversaw the operation. After the operation, Prime Minister Thatcher went to the base of the SAS soldiers to congratulate them. She praised their success and professionalism and thanked them. Thatcher's behaviour was an exemplar of a decision maker who stands behind the men who take great risk in serving their country.

It was one of these hostage rescue scenarios that Margaret Thatcher was asked to take part in the 80's while visiting an SAS regiment. While other VIPs and dignitaries visiting the SAS have only begrudgingly accepted this offer, the Iron Lady jumped at the chance and insisted on being the hostage. Her bodyguard, George advised against this, prompting an annoyed Thatcher to suggest that if he was so worried about her safety around the most elite fighting force the country she ran had at its disposal, he should accompany her. a few minutes later Thatcher and her bodyguard were huddled into a room, sat at a table flanked by cardboard targets, and were then left there in total darkness. A few minutes later an SAS operative kicked down the door, hurled a flashbang grenade through the hole, fired two rounds into every target and then hit the lights. When the smoke cleared the SAS, operatives gathered were stunned to see Thatcher sat at total ease absentmindedly resting her hands on the table beside her purse. George on the other hand had responded to the hail of bullets by leaping under the table and cowering in a puddle of his fear urine. Prompting an irate Thatcher to, according to the SAS, say "Get up George, you're embarrassing me. assuming George later tried to explain his cowardice by stating he was trying to protect Thatcher's legs!

Operation Nimrod was just five days after the failed rescue attempt at the American Embassy in downtown Teheran by the US special forces.

Chapter 10: The Pirates

War ... always has been a matter of profit and spoils. What is changing is how the profits are distributed.

Piracy in Somalia is a highly organized, lucrative, ransom-driven business. pirates hijacked ships, and in many cases, they were paid million-dollar ransoms to release them. The juicy payoffs have attracted gunmen from across Somalia, and the pirates are thought to number in the thousands. The piracy industry started about 10 to 15 years ago, as a response to illegal fishing. Somalia's central government imploded in 1991, casting the country into chaos. With no patrols along the shoreline, Somalia's tuna-rich waters were soon plundered by commercial fishing fleets from around the world. Somali fishermen armed themselves and turned into vigilantes by confronting illegal fishing boats and demanding that they pay a tax.

"From there, they got greedy," "They started attacking everyone." By the early 2000s, many of the fishermen had traded in their nets for machine guns and were hijacking any vessel they could catch: sailboat, oil tanker, United Nations-chartered food ship. "It's true that the pirates started to defend the fishing business,". "And illegal fishing is a real problem for them. But this does not justify these boys to now act like guardians. They are criminals. The world must help crack down on them." The United States and several European countries, in particular France, have been talking about ways to patrol the waters together. The United Nations is even considering something like a maritime peacekeeping force. Because of all the hijackings, the waters off Somalia's coast are considered the most dangerous shipping lanes in the world.

Mogadishu one of the world's most stunning monuments to conflict: block after block, mile after mile, of scorched, gutted-out buildings. Mogadishu's architecture, once a gem along the Indian Ocean, has been reduced to a pile of machine-gunned bricks. Somalia has been ripped apart by violence since the central government imploded in 1991. Eighteen years and 14 failed attempts at a government later, the killing goes on and on and on, suicide bombs, white phosphorus bombs, beheadings, medieval-style stoning's, teenage troops high on the local drug called khat blasting away at each other and anything in between. It is the same violent free-for-all on the seas. Somalia's pirates are choking off one of the most strategic waterways in the world, the Gulf of Aden. These heavily armed buccaneers hijacked ships. It is the greatest piracy epidemic of modern times.

Somalia is unified on the surface, poisonously divided beneath. It is one of the world's most homogeneous nation-states, with nearly all its estimated 10 million people sharing the same language, the same religion, the same culture, and the same ethnicity. But in Somalia, it is all about clan. Somalis divide themselves into several clans, subclans, sub-subclans, with shifting allegiances that have bedevilled outsiders for years.

The rate of piracy incidents off the Horn of Africa has escalated considerably since 2005 and severely over the last year, as both the quantity and the size and value of the vessels attacked and taken for ransom has escalated exponentially. Predictably, this escalation tracks and reflects significant advancements in the organization of Somali piracy. What began as mere "maritime muggings" has evolved into sophisticated, adaptive, and multifaceted international organized crime. The average attack is launched by a cell of 10 armed pirates typically divided into three fast boats and led by an offshore chief with ties to a clan-based warlord on land. The boats are generally high-tech, made of fiberglass, and powered by 40-50 horsepower outboard engines. The pirates are kitted with grappling hooks and aluminium ladders, rocket-propelled grenades, rifles, knives, narcotics, satellite phones, global positioning systems, Generally, targets are lured in using deceptive tactics such as phony distress calls or pirates posing as fishermen. Vessels are fired upon and compelled to slow their speed of approach while pirates' clamour aboard, commandeer the ship, and sail it to anchorage off a friendly coastal town such as Eyl. Five and six figure ransoms are then negotiated while crews and cargo are held for lengthy periods. Pirates rarely harm their hostages. While pirates are currently using coastal cities such as Eyl to launch their operations, they in fact require little infrastructure to do so. The pirates easily launch their boats from beaches. convoying merchant vessels is a more effective use of resources for navies, but as the risk of falling prey to the pirates is still relatively low, the shipping industry will continue to find it an economically inefficient and impractical way to respond, preferring to pay the ransoms once the risk materialises. The homeland of most of the pirates is the autonomous region known as Puntland—from Cape Guardafui on the tip of the Horn down from the Gulf of Aden along the Indian Ocean coast past the town of Eyl. there, during a faltering and unstable economy, piracy has become an industry.

Arming merchant vessels undertaken in different ways. One option is to put armed security teams' aboard vessels. A second, and more controversial option, is to arm merchant crews. The first option is already undertaken especially if the ship is considered high risk. stationing security teams aboard all vessels would not be cost efficient. The second option – arming merchant crews has largely been rejected by shipping companies and port-authorities. The added security risks, costs, and legal liability are deemed too high.

The reason no military action against pirates has yet been undertaken ashore stems from political will rather than legal constraints. UN Security Council Resolution 1851 in fact authorises military action against piracy on Somali territory. If the piracy problem persists or even worsens however, such escalatory steps may become increasingly more plausible. Military action ashore could range from small raids against pirate equipment to larger scale, sustained military operations. Neither will be risk free. Pirates even see their work as nationalistic. One of the Pirates of Puntland, Mr Ali, noted: "We don't consider ourselves sea bandits.... We consider sea bandits those who illegally fish in our seas and dump waste in our seas and carry weapons in our seas. We are simply patrolling our seas. Think of us like a coast guard." In the past, these pirates have been content to board ships and steal their cargo, such as oil from tankers. However, this activity has reduced, speculating that the slide in oil prices has made such crime less attractive. Instead, the gangs now tend to board vessels up to 120 nautical miles offshore, kidnap some of the crew and take them ashore to be held for ransom. Somalia pirates kidnapped 24 crew members in the first half of this year, up from just 10 in the first six months of 2020.These incidents are “increasingly violent”, with Somalia accounting for eight of the nine incidents worldwide in which ships were fired on in the January. Even though paying a ransom is likely to encourage further kidnappings, they were always paid. "It's exceedingly difficult to imagine a ship-owner who is prepared to ignore the plight of his kidnapped crew members. It would be very unlikely to happen. You can't abandon them".

Chapter 11: Who will pay?

If everyone does not pay the price to win, then everyone will pay the price of losing.

QSS are ship-owners that are compelled to pay ransoms to Somali pirates, Qatar Subsea Services, the diving division of Halul Offshore Services Company, acquired from Qatar Navigation in 2001. QSS originally formed in 1998 and is now one of the largest marine & diving support companies in the region. John Alden, Diving Operations Dept. QSS offer complete in house ROV pipeline inspection surveys utilizing soft data & video acquisitioning software in conjunction with Seaeye cougar ROV. Now the company is part of Milaha group, the diving department expanded to 4 permanent diving vessels, 2 air and 2 saturation all with ROV capabilities. Milaha Offshore is a provider of a wide spread of world-class offshore support services, with a presence extending from the Middle East to Europe, Africa, and South East Asia.

Milaha Offshore owns and operates a fleet of over 75 high specification offshore support vessels across the service spectrum to support Marine, Exploration & Drilling, Production, EPIC, Maintenance, Jack-up Accommodation, Rig-less Well Intervention, Stimulation, Diving & Survey and Sub-sea intervention. The fleet also includes anchor handling and supply vessels, safety standby boats, workboats, crew boats, and dynamic positioning (DP) vessels, allowing us to provide a complete range of diving services including saturation diving. Milaha also owns and operates the most advanced offshore maintenance, diving, and underwater inspection equipment such as Remotely Operated Vehicles (ROVs). The size and diversity of Milaha's modern fleet and the unique breadth of services are structured to provide End to End support. But one thing is clear ship-owners are compelled to pay ransoms to Somali pirates for the release of their vessels and crew. Moreover, it is intolerable that safe passage cannot be guaranteed through some of the world's principal shipping lanes. All absent intervention by states, a ship owner who has his ship hijacked has no option but to pay a ransom. Much is rightly written about preventative measures that can be deployed to avoid being hijacked, but once you are caught, the game is up.

They Refuse to negotiate or refuse to pay. You will not get your ship and crew back; Rely on your national military or private military, there seems no appetite for a risky military solution once a vessel has reached the Somali coast and a private military solution is impractical and illegal; or negotiate and pay a ransom. this is your only move; your only hope of securing the release of your crew and your vessel. often you hear calls to ban ransom payments to outlaw the only method a shipowner has to remove his crew from harm's way and rescue his vessel, calls to ban ransom payments come from people who have little knowledge of the shipping industry and the issues at stake. But worryingly, the calls sometimes also come from well-intentioned politicians who wield real influence.

If a shipowner is prohibited from paying a ransom, the consequences are First, we condemn the seafarers held hostage to an ugly and uncertain future. In debriefs John has undertaken following the release of vessels, evidence from seafarers who have been subjected to degrading treatment, humiliating treatment, torture, and from seafarers who witnessed the death and execution of their fellow hostages. This will be their future. vessels and cargo will be lost. This loss will fall on the shipowners. If the US,

European Union passes a law which bans ransom payments, which they might people have to question whether such a law would violate the Convention on Human Rights. Would outlawing the only viable method of removing a seafarer from harm's way not be in breach the right to life and the right to freedom from torture, inhumane and degrading treatment?

Ban Ransom payments and It would take time before the message got through to the pirates that no more money could be paid. If we consider the current average length of detention, such lead time is probably going to be more than nine months. Statistics suggest that by then, a further 35 ships would be captured, and a further 750 seafarers held captive. some shipowners will have the support of their governments and crown immunity. These shipowners will continue to pay. Their ships and crew will continue to be released. The pirates will not then believe that some shipowners cannot pay, and the pirates will not be discouraged from capturing more ships. We will have a two-tier system with one tier of shipowners having to witness the sacrifice of their crew and vessels, while others are released.

The support the UK government's stance that it does not and should not pay ransoms. John believes in supporting private individuals' rights to act within the law to resolve a kidnapping and hijacking on commercial terms. If the international community is to continue to sit by and allow pirates to hijack vessels it would be unconscionable for lawmakers to take away a shipowner's only prospect of rescuing its personnel and assets, good intentions or wrong, of Puntland's President Abdirahaman Mohamud Farole to ban the payment of ransoms, QSS will not pay and the British government will not pay! The government won't pay but they will solve the issue in their own, very British way by sending in the Royal Marines, as they have done for the last few hundred years.

Green Lidded Steely Eyed Killers we all love and know, The Royal Marines. The history of the Royal Marines began on 28 October 1664.They are not the oldest Marine Unit in the World, that honour goes to the Spanish, Infantería de Marina (1537), the Fanti da Mar of the Republic of Venice (1550), the Portuguese Marine Corps (1610) and France's Troupes de marine (1622). The 'first official' unit of English naval infantry, originally called the Duke of York and Albany's Maritime Regiment of Foot and soon becoming known as the Admiral's Regiment, was formed on 28 October 1664, with an initial strength of 1,200 infantrymen recruited from the Trained Bands of London as part of the mobilisation for the Second Anglo-Dutch War. James (later King James VII & II), the Duke of York and Albany, Lord High Admiral, and brother of King Charles II, was Captain-General of the Artillery Company, now the Honourable Artillery Company.

It consisted of six 200-man companies and was initially commanded by Colonel Sir William Killigrew with Sir Charles Lyttleton as lieutenant-colonel. Killigrew had commanded an English regiment in Dutch service, and many of the regiment's initial complement of officers had served there as well. The Holland Regiment (later The Buffs) was also raised to serve at sea and both "Naval" regiments were paid for by the Treasurer of the Navy by Order of Council of 11 July 1665. John Churchill, later the 1st Duke of Marlborough, was a famous member of this regiment. A Company of Foot Guards served as Marines to augment the Marines of the Admiral's Regiment during the key sea battle the Battle of Solebay in 1672. The regiment was disbanded in 1689 shortly after James II was deposed in the Glorious Revolution. Two marine regiments of the army were raised in 1690. They were the Earl of Pembroke's and Torrington's, later Lord Berkeley's. These two regiments participated in an opposed landing during the Williamite War in Ireland at Cork, Ireland on 21 September 1690 under the command of John Churchill, now the Duke of Marlborough.

Chapter 12: Help Somalia.

largest single fire fight since Vietnam

The U.S. gave relatively little attention to Somalia until 1992 when the human suffering brought on by famine and fighting became headline news. American was focused on defeating Iraq in the Gulf War and on dealing with the aftermath of this defeat. The U.S. was more concerned with executing Operation Provide Comfort in Northern Iraq, addressing the potential nuclear threat in North Korea, deciding its role in the former Yugoslavia, deciding what NATO's role should be in the post-Cold War era, and using the Gulf War as a catalyst to bring about an improved peace agreement in the Middle East.

On 4 May 1993, the United Nations Operation Somalia II took over responsibility II's mandate included the ambitious task of nation building while before had only been responsible for providing the conditions necessary for the distribution of humanitarian aid. organization and force levels, to assume the mission it was given, II had less combat power to impose its will on the warlords, and its staff was new and undermanned. Furthermore, planning, coordination, and implementation would be more difficult since not all the forces had worked together. Yet, they embarked upon a path that would lead them into direct conflict with Aideed; a confrontation that the leaders, Ambassador Robert Oakley, and

Lieutenant General Robert Johnston, had felt wise to avoid, even with their larger force and unified command. Tension began to increase almost immediately between UNOSOM II and Aideed's Somalia National Alliance (SNA).

They tried to isolate and marginalize Aideed from the start. Concerned with Aideed's vitriol, Lieutenant General Bir directed some of his staff to develop some options as to how to shut down Aideed's radio station. With civilian Somali spies throughout UNOSOMII headquarters, it is likely that Aideed knew the UN was making plans to harm his organization. So, when Pakistani forces on short notice arrived on 5 June 1993 to conduct authorized arms inspections at the SNA arms cache collocated at the radio station and other locations, Aideed may have believed that the Pakistanis were there to shut down his radio station, a major source of his power. As a result of these fears, a desire to confront the UN, or both, Aideed ordered his SNA forces to conduct a series of coordinated attacks against the Pakistanis. In these actions, Aideed's forces killed 24 and wounded 57 Pakistani troops and wounded one Italian and three American soldiers.

On 6 June 1993, the United Nations Security Council unanimously passed Resolution #837 which basically declared war on Aideed in all but name. The resolution called for the investigation and prosecution of the individuals responsible for the Pakistani ambushes. UNOSOM II had thus transitioned from its neutral role in peace enforcement to taking sides and fighting a counter-insurgency campaign. UN Ambassador Madeleine K. Albright, in consultation with Anthony (Tony) Lake and Ambassador Howe, hastily drew up the resolution. GEN Colin Powell was not consulted. The National Security Council principals never discussed the policy implications of this resolution for U.S. involvement in Somalia. The resolution would basically commit U.S. forces to fighting a counter-insurgency.

Even so, Howe had the choice of how to implement the resolution since Aideed was not mentioned by name in the resolution. The day after the 5 June 93 SNA ambush of the Pakistanis, Howe began lobbying his old boss Anthony Lake, President Clinton's National Security Advisor, for the Delta Force to be sent to capture Aideed. He originally envisioned a small force that would deploy secretly and capture Aideed while he was still out in the open. Failing to get Pentagon support for Delta, on 12 June 1993 Howe and Bir attempted to destroy Aideed's capabilities through three days of AC-130H, AH-1 helicopter attacks, and QRF raids on his acknowledged and unacknowledged weapon storage sites, chop shops containing thirty "technicals," and radio station. The U.S. supplied the assets and support to conduct these attacks. This phase of military operations against the SNA ended on 17 June 1993 when another significant escalation occurred. Here UNOSOM II mounted a major early morning cordon and search operation that nearly resulted in the capture of Aideed. The SNA warlord escaped by having his forces conduct a diversionary attack on the perimeter. SNA conducted part of the attack from Digfer Hospital, a suspected but undeclared SNA weapons storage site. UNOSOM II forces returned fire on the SNA snipers on top of the hospital. But, in doing so, UNOSOM II damaged its own legitimacy in the eyes of the international press. Press coverage of the collateral damage from the U.S. supplied AC-130s used in the operation led to the gunships' recall from theatre. After failing to capture Aideed on 17 June 1993, Howe, with the concurrence of Lieutenant General Bir, Force Commander, UNOSOMII, and his deputy and Commander of U.S. Forces Somalia, Major General Thomas Montgomery, posted a twenty-five-thousand-dollar reward for information leading to the capture of Aideed. In retrospect, the reward had the opposite effect to that which it was intended to have. SNA members considered the UN reward an insult because it was so small. The reward reinforced what Aideed told his clan members: the UN was interfering in Somalia's internal struggle. Instead of weakening Aideed, the small reward further unified Somali support for Aideed. The U.S.'s redeployment of the AC-130Hs effectively gave Aideed another victory. The U.S. had in effect backed down by removing its biggest and most feared weapon.

Without the psychological and military effect of the AC-130Hs, Howe decided that UNOSOM II forces should keep a low profile in Mogadishu and wait to see the effect of his award. Meanwhile, Howe continued to lobby his contacts in Washington, D.C. for Delta to be sent. Many critics of UNOSOM II' s performance believe that Howe made a mistake by putting a small reward on Aideed's head and then waiting to see the impact of this reward. Instead, critics contend that Howe should have used his position of strength after conducting the impressive 17 June 1993 cordon and search mission to get Aideed to negotiate. Aideed was on the run and feeling the pressure of UNOSOM II. He had lost a significant amount of his arms and was afraid of the AC-130s.

Instead, UNOSOMII forces hunkered down and waited for the reward to produce Aideed. The elusive warlord, for his part, became more aggressive as UNOSOM remained more passive. UNOSOM became so focused on capturing Aideed that it was not able to focus on its political reconciliation tasks. UNOSOM II had effectively become isolated in southern Mogadishu. By the beginning of July Aideed had started to increase the number of aggressive actions: ambushes, vehicular mines, helicopter attacks, rocket propelled Grenade (RPG) rounds fired, and mortar rounds fired.

While UNOSOM II commanders waited, they faced a unity of effort problem with their contributing nations. Italy and Pakistan, two of the largest contributors to UNOSOM II, were satisfied with the amount of retribution paid to the SNA. Disagreement over the largely U.S. and Boutros Boutros-Ghali supported hunt for Aideed prevented UNOSOM II from achieving the needed unity of command and effort. Italian forces ultimately made separate peace with Aideed and the SNA.

Howe rejected the idea of any resolution in Somalia including a criminal like Aideed. So, Howe continued in his efforts to seek additional forces to capture Aideed or to destroy his organization with the forces that were available to him. When the decision to send TFR to Somalia was first discussed in June 93, Ambassador Howe advised the National Command Authority (NCA) that the special operations force had a ninety percent chance of capturing General Aideed. Ambassador Howe's assessment was based upon the situation at that time; Aideed was not in hiding and UNOSOM II had not attempted to capture him. So, Howe believed that a small special operations unit could have easily conducted a covert night operation to capture a sleeping and unsuspecting Aideed. Powell and Hoar resisted any such deployment and were supported by the White House.

In the meantime, Howe thought he had a chance to eliminate the most radical of Aideed's clan while they met in an SNA headquarters building known as the Abdi House on 12 July 1993. SNA moderates were supposed to be meeting at a different building at the same time. Without any warning, Cobra helicopters fired 11 TOW missiles into the building and killed between 20 and 215 according to the International Red Cross.

This UNOSOMII escalation had several unintended consequences. First, it caused the Italians to threaten to pull out of UNOSOM II. Second, instead of destroying Aideed's organization, it greatly strengthened it. Clan moderates and intellectuals who had supported a negotiated settlement with UNOSOM II were now firmly behind Aideed against UNOSOM II. Third, the SNA increased its combat operations against the UN, specifically Americans. Thus, the attack against the Abdi House was a major turning point for UNOSOM II and the next step in the escalation that would lead to the deployment of TFR.

By 8 August 1993 it was evident that the SNA were focusing its attacks on Americans; Aideed had successfully used command-detonated mines to kill four Americans. SNA command detonated mines wounded four more Americans on 19 August 1993. Two days later, on 21 August 1993, GEN Powell called Secretary Aspin and reluctantly recommended that the TFR be sent to Somalia. Powell was reluctant to send TFR because he understood the risk involved in conducting such mission. Powell felt that something had to be done given the increasing casualties inflicted by the SNA. 45 With Powell's opposition lifted, approval was swift. Aspin concurred along with Warren Christopher and Anthony Lake. When Lake notified President Clinton the next day about the deployment, he did not object. 46 Aspin, however, "urged [Powell] that at the same time the visibility of the U.S. effort should be reduced." Powell interpreted this to mean that TFR should be kept to the minimum force required. This was the guidance given to GEN Downing. MG Garrison advised GEN Downing that the mission could be accomplished without the AC-130s and the extra platoon for local security. MG Garrison had not requested the AC-13 Os during the time he had been in Somalia. Since GEN Hoar was against the deployment from the beginning, he advocated sending only the necessary forces required to do the mission, no more no less. The extra platoon for local security was outside the mission requirements of Task Force Ranger because local security was the responsibility of the Allies. By the time TFR was ordered to Somalia in the end of August 1993, the situation in Mogadishu had completely changed. Aideed was in hiding and knew TFR was in Mogadishu to capture him. By some accounts he was moving every two hours, changing his means of travel, wearing disguises, sleeping at a different location each night. To deal with the increased threat, GEN Downing recommended a larger force that included the deployed TFR, AC-130s, and an extra ground reaction platoon.

When the National Command Authority approved the mission based upon the recommendation of General Powell, it did so with the understanding that while TFR was conducting a high-risk operation in trying to capture Aideed there was no possibility of a catastrophic failure. The NCA supported the continuation of the missions without a serious reassessment of risks after each mission. What is apparent from this background narrative is that TFR's deployment was the last in a series of steps taken by the Clinton Administration to salvage the ambitious U.N. led mission in Somalia. The decision to deploy TFR had its roots in the Administration's support of UNSCR #837, which all but called for Aideed's arrest by name for ambushing the Pakistanis, and in its desire to limit resources for the Somali problem. As UNOSOM II proved itself not up to the task of confronting and capturing Aideed, the Administration, in the face of increasing casualties, decided to give TFR a try. The major policy problem was that the TFR's military actions were uncoordinated with any diplomatic effort. And as the next section of the paper will show, the military force alone was too little, too late.

What happened on 3-4 October 1993 Having discussed the events leading up to the deployment of TFR, it is time to describe the TFR raid itself, specifically, the events leading to the successful Somali attack on Crash Site #2. The timing of the events is important to determine if additional tanks and APCs could have prevented Crash Site #2 from being overrun and, thus, precluded the failure of the TFR mission. Understanding what happened is a prerequisite for determining the nature of the failure and identifying the critical failures. With ominous foreshadowing in late September 1993, MG Garrison Commander of Task Force Ranger, predicted, "If we go into the vicinity of the Bakara Market, there's no question we'll win the gunfight. But we might lose the war."

In its seventh raid since arriving in country on 26 August 1993 with the mission to capture Aideed, TFR launched a raid on a building in the heart of "Indian country," three miles from the TFR compound at the Mogadishu airport and near the Olympic Hotel in the vicinity of the same Bakara market that Garrison knew posed a great threat. To compensate for the inherent risks of conducting a daylight raid in Aideed's own backyard, Garrison for the first time "ordered his AH-6 "littlebird" attack helicopters to carry rockets as well to shoot any threatening Somali gunman rather than give them a chance to surrender." Garrison knew how fast the Somalis had reacted to his previous six missions. He planned to further reduce risk by being on the target for only about one hour, speed equalled security.

At 1300 MG Garrison received actionable intelligence from a Somali agent. The TFR's spy reported that Aideed's lieutenants would be meeting in a building on Hawlwadig Road a block over from the Olympic Hotel near the Bakara market, a densely populated SNA controlled area. The target house remained under constant surveillance, video, and photography, by OH 58 helicopter and P-3 Orion spy plane as TFR prepared for the mission. At 1540 two AH-6 gunships flew over the target building for the final check. Immediately after this, four MH-6's touched down close to the building long enough for 16 delta soldiers to jump off and assault the target. Two MH-60 helicopters dropped off 30 more special operations soldiers to conduct close-in security and assist the assault team. Five minutes later four more MH-60 helicopters, carrying about sixteen Rangers each, arrived to provide outer security. Chalk One was led by 1LT Larry Perino, and CPT Mike

Steele fast roped in at the southeast road intersection closest to the target building. Chalk Two led by 1LT Tom DiTomasso's fast roped in at the northeast road intersection closest to the target building. Chalk Three led by SFC Sean Watson fast roped in on Hawlwadig Road at the southwest road intersection. While still in the helicopter, Chalk Four started to receive fire. An RPG round exploded near the MH-60. Under fire SGT Matt Eversmann had his Chalk Four fast rope in about a block too far north of its intended drop point at the northwest comer road intersection. One of the rangers (PFC Blackburn) in Chalk Four missed the rope and crashed to the ground. Rangers started receiving fire almost immediately, earlier than in previous missions. The ground convoy led by LTC McKnight arrived at the target building to load up the prisoners. LTC McKnight ordered that Blackburn be evacuated back to base, which should have been a five-minute drive with a cargo HMMWV, and two guns mounted HMMWVs to provide security. The column successfully fought through ambushes to save Blackburn, but another soldier (SGT Dominick Pilla) was killed in the process. Meanwhile, Chalk 4 had taken three more casualties, in addition to Blackburn, from the growing number of attacking Somalis.

Soon after Blackburn's medical evacuation convoy departed and the 24 prisoners started to get loaded in LTC McKnight's vehicle convoy, a MH-60 designated Super 61 was shot down at 1620 by an RPG and crashed about 300 yards from the target house. Super 61 had just finished trying to provide fire support with its on-board snipers when it was hit by the RPG. Half of 1LT DiTomasso's Chalk Two and part of Chalk One ran to secure the crash site. During the movement several were wounded (1 seriously - dies at 20:27 at Crash Site #1) and one was killed. 1LT DiTomasso's squad arrived at the crash site just after an MH-6 landed at Crash Site #1 to recover two wounded in action (WIA), the two pilots were killed in the crash (one of the WIA later died of wounds).

DiTomasso's re-established a perimeter around Super 61 to allow the wounded to be evacuated on the MH-6 and prevent Somali's from desecrating the bodies of the two dead pilots. Super 62 provided security overhead. Meanwhile at 16:26, the Joint Operations Centre (JOC) ordered the ground reaction force (GRF1), (LTC McKnight) to move with the assault force and prisoners to Crash Site #1 to collect the rest of his unit and the bodies of the dead pilots. (CSAR Team, DiTomasso's Chalk, CPT Steele's Chalk, and Delta soldiers total about 90)

Super 68 arrived at Crash Site #1 at 16:28 with the combat search and rescue (CSAR) team. In the process, Super 68 was hit by an RPG and returned immediately to base. Approximately 90 soldiers moved to secure Crash Site #1 while the CSAR team extracted only one of the dead pilots from the wreckage-the other could not be removed without additional equipment. The Somalis continued to conduct persistent attacks on the security perimeter while soldiers and helicopters kept them back until the relief column arrived the next morning. At 16:29, the 10th Mountain Quick Reaction Force (QRF) company was directed to depart the university compound and conduct a link up with TFR at the airport. To get there, the QRF was ordered to take a long route to avoid SNA controlled areas. This took until 17:24, nearly an hour.

Meanwhile LTC McKnight began moving with his assault force, prisoners, and convoy to Crash Site #1 about 4 blocks away. Although Crash Site #1 was only 300 yards away, LTC McKnight had not seen where the first helicopter had gone down and needed the assistance of the P3 Orion to direct the convoy to Crash Site #1 to secure the rest of his force. Before he could get to the first crash site, the Somalis used RPGs to shoot down a third helicopter, Super 64, as it orbited to provide fire support for Crash Site #1. At 16:40, Super 64 crashed about a half-mile south of Crash Site #1. The two pilots and crewmembers survived the crash and proceeded to set up security in the hope that help would soon arrive. Now, McKnight was directed to rescue the soldiers at Crash Site #2 after completing the same task at Crash Site #1. This may seem easy by the distances alone, but McKnight was receiving time-delayed directions from the P3, when seconds counted. He was not able to talk directly to the P3 crewmember giving directions. As a result, he kept missing the correct turn. Further complicating the route to the Crash Site #1 was the fact that the P3 was giving him directions that would help him avoid various roadblocks the SNA and Somalis were emplacing. In addition, McKnight had not told any of his other drivers where he was going so that if the lead vehicle got hit the convoy could continue. Confusing, late directions were compounded by steady, persistent attacks by the Somalis with rifles and RPGs -- especially when the convoy crossed any road intersection. Fog and friction were directly impacting on mission accomplishment. After 45 minutes of wandering through the hostile streets of the SNA, McKnight ended up - in front of the Olympic Hotel with too many casualties and too many damaged vehicles to successfully reach crash site. This convoy would finally make it back to the airfield with many wounded, four killed in action (KIA) and three Somali prisoners killed. Black hawk down.

Chapter 13: Life as a Hostage

We are looking for bodies, and we're looking for a hostage taker.

John made a vow to himself that while he was a hostage that if lucky enough to live and to get out of Somalia, he would do something meaningful with his life - and specifically something that would be meaningful. It is quite easy to have hope when the situation inclines the lads to, when they are given good news. It could be a hand gesture or a word that slips out in Arabic – "your situation is simple, Insha'Allah (God willing), everything is going to be alright." It could also be an explanation of the operations of the organization that was holding them, a nationalist pirate group. a guard dressed as a policeman came to tell john how his group operated: "We capture, we judge the hostages, and then we divide them up into two compartments, the execution compartment and the negotiation compartment." And he added this sentence with nearly saving grace: "You are in the right compartment, patience is beautiful, as the proverb says, you will be set free one of these days."

John realized that, over time, their resistance capacities had not been worn down too much. When free, Men very rarely test their resistance capacities, especially mental capacities. But they exist; man can confront terrible ordeals. They spent the first two weeks without brushing their teeth or taking a shower. They survived. Confusedly, they had gotten over one resistance hurdle. being transferred lying down in a sort of cardboard coffin, hidden under blankets, blindfolded with their hands tied behind our backs, in the back of a car driving along unsafe roads. they were also confronted with combat between the guerrillas and American soldiers around the house where they were being held. they followed the orders given and laid down on blankets, keeping away from the windows, which were obstructed to keep them from being located. And then, after one big scare and another big scare, the storm subsided. They could handle the ordeals. The Divers almost felt strong. at least capable of taking the bad news that we could receive at any time – because that is the fate of all hostages.

For days, they lived face to face with death. Every metallic noise that john heard coming from the room next to them had the divers thinking that the pirate captors were getting the block ready. They barely spoke anymore when they brought meals. Hope was gone. faces were frozen. The pressure was so strong that john could hear his heartbeat. They moved the mattresses together to feel less alone. John stared at the wall three meters in front of him. As bodies grew numb. Strangely, not his head, which hurt. It was his stomach. He had knots in his stomach. Bloodcurdling anguish he could feel the knots inside. lost his appetite. and imagined his own death. He felt like they were on a death ride, slowly, the end of life was coming. And yet, accepting to die was an affront and need to fight against a tragic fate.

When hope is taken away, people absolutely must create hope. Otherwise, they collapse. Right from the start, John kept this principle in mind: in a difficult situation, but he is British, he had to keep hoping, keep cool, imagine that he was back in the Marines on a rough trip for two or three days." Why two or four days? That was how long it was the last time he was held; he had been taken prisoner a few years earlier in Argentina.

Survival also entails being in fairly good shape physically. That is why, as soon as they could, the Divers got some exercise. They stretched as much as they could, legs, torsos, lifted weights, did pushups, shook out hands, heads. One hour every day on a one-square-meter mat. In the end, they realized they could keep in shape without many accessories. Moving, running around a ten-square-meter room would wear them out, giving them the same sensations as after jogging, Exercise gave a link to normal life.

The lads found cohesion that despair had not taken away, even though the anguish of death had made them nearly silent toward one and other. Johno is not very talkative in general. Until last week, he had been optimistic. John was also optimistic, while playing the devil's advocate. "What if this drags on?" He said at the beginning of the captivity. "And what if they bring up the subject of Money?" John was, and still is, an anxious optimist. Johno seemed to John to be almost casually optimistic, until the 28th of February, when he flinched when confronted with the serious threat that was now hanging over them. Strangely, John was the one who played the role of social worker at this point. kept telling Johno that a dead hostage is of no value, that after days of negotiations, the pirates had no reason to throw the baby out with the bathwater, that they had to handle the latest crisis, the latest bluff, the latest attempt by the pirates to force the negotiators' hands before a happy ending. Once again, John was looking for reasons to hope, so as not to lose it completely. Speaking Arabic, being able to talk a little bit with our captors, trying to understand their motivations, guessing how things were going, all this of course helped greatly. As did the fact that there were two of former Marines. Especially two friends, together in their ordeal, being able to give each other mutual support. When there are two of you, the bad news hurts but you can share it. Alone, you are cruelly so in the face of the despair that a mate can help you to handle. They lived captivity as a challenge. There was no way they could give up. This sort of ordeal is extremely hard to bear. But deep within, each of them has unimaginable resources to overcome the most dangerous situations.

Past experiences with Internment, John Starts to remember the drills he got taught on the SAS Survival course back in 1985: dealing with someone intent on negotiating for what they really want, an internment period will follow. This may last a few hours, a few days, or even weeks. This is the time when negotiations are taking place and the time to do some planning for various contingencies. During this time, hostages like john knows he must employ the "3

C's." **Calm** Stay as calm as you can. When hostages panic, hostage-takers panic, and the situation can escalate beyond the hostage-takers original intentions. You can appear calm by following directions and avoiding sensitive topics in any conversation with the hostage-taker. **Connect**, by appearing to empathize (not sympathize) with your captor, you will become a person to them rather than a brokering chip. In some cases, by creating a bond, hostages have reversed the Stockholm syndrome, making captors unwilling to harm their captives. By connecting, you buy yourself time by slowing things down. Encourage the negotiation process and keep the focus on outside contact. **Capitalize**, while encouraging a negotiated release or some other peaceful conclusion, remain alert to rescue efforts and escape opportunities. Resolution Research indicates that 80 percent of all hostages worldwide survive their ordeal one way or another. Resolutions are typically characterized by one of three options: Negotiated Release – A negotiated release is the safest and sometimes longest outcome, requiring patience and calmness from all involved. Rescue – Success of a rescue operation depends on the rescuer's ability to distinguish between the hostages and the hostage-taker. Cooperation of the hostages is critical. Avoid being misconstrued as the criminal by avoiding threatening posture. Do not grab and hold on to the weapon, and make sure the rescuers can see your empty hands (sometimes the good guys must put their hands up. If you are not sure what to do, stay low until instructed to proceed. Escape – Escape is the riskiest resolution. If an opportunity presents itself and the risk of not escaping is greater, take it. Recognize that you are betting with your life. If at any time your hostage-taker develops into a shooter, instructions to get out or take out.

John and the lads know their value to those who are holding them is only if alive, and they want to keep them that way. their best defence is passive cooperation. The more time passes, the better chances of being released alive. The best opportunity for escape was in the beginning, during the confusion of the apprehension while still onboard the DSV. Escape though was impossible, too risky. Now they had to plan an escape.

John and the divers quickly settled into the situation. became observant. Noticed the details of the room, the sounds of activity in the building and determined the layout of the building by studying what is visible. Listened for sounds through walls, windows and out in the streets, they tried to distinguish between smells. Noted the number, names, physical description, accents, habits, and rank structure of the pirates. They tried to memorize this information so they could report it after they eventually got released. Memorized their schedule, looked for patterns of behaviour to be used to advantage, and identified weaknesses, vulnerabilities. Used this information to assess opportunities to escape. Expected to be accused of being an intelligence agent and to be interrogated intensively. Did not admit to any accusations. Keep answers short and did not volunteer information or make unnecessary overtures. John and his team established a rapport with the pirates. Family is a universal subject. So are sports and many hobbies. The goal to get the pirates to view them as a real people, rather than simply an object. Listen actively to the pirate's feelings and concerns, never praise, participate in, or debate their "cause." If john knew' Somali, the pirate's language and used it. Asking them to teach all the lads their language. Speaking normally. Not complaining. Avoided being belligerent and complied with all orders and instructions. Once a level of rapport or communication was achieved, tried asking for items that would increase personal comfort. John was not afraid to ask for anything needed and wanted such as medicines, books, papers. Made requests in a reasonable, low-key manner. Planned on a lengthy stay and devised a way to keep track of the passage of time. They approximated time by noting changes in temperature between night and day, the frequency and intensity of outside noises (traffic, birds), and by observing the alertness of the pirates. Established a daily schedule of mental as well as physical exercise. used isometric and flexing exercises to keep muscles toned. To maintain strength, eating what given even if it did not look appetising, which it did not. Used relaxation techniques to reduce stress. If they detected the presence of other hostages in the same building, tried ways to communicate. During interrogation, did not become uncooperative, antagonistic, or hostile towards the pirates. People who display this type of behaviour are often held longer or become the object of torture or punishment. They took a simple, tenable position and stuck to it. Being polite and kept their temper. Gave short answers. Talked freely about nonessential matters but guarded when conversations turn to matters of substance. Didn't get lulled by a friendly approach. Remembered, one terrorist may play "Good Guy" and one "Bad Guy." This is the most common interrogation technique. Established a friendly rapport but maintained personal dignity and did not compromise their integrity. When forced to present terrorist demands to authorities, in writing, stated clearly that the demands are from the pirates. Avoided making a plea on their own behalf. Very patient, as the hostage negotiations were difficult and time consuming. Remembered, their chances of survival increase with time. Most episodes of hostage-taking end with no loss of life or physical injury to the captive. Eventually they will probably be released or rescued. So did not try to escape. When an attempt was made to rescue John and the group, they kept a low profile and immediately followed all instructions. Rescue attempted only after negotiations had failed. That means that lives of hostages, pirates, and rescue forces are all at risk during the rescue. John didn't want to be shot in the confusion while the rescue team identifies the pirates, who tried to disguise themselves as hostages. To protect the team, John told the divers: DO NOT RUN. Drop to the floor and remain still. If not possible, bow their heads, and stand still. Make no sudden moves that a tense rescuer may interpret as hostile. Wait for instructions and obey all instructions given. Do not be upset if a rescuer isn't sure whether you are a terrorist or hostage. Even if you are handcuffed and searched, do not resist. Just wait for the confusion to clear.

Chapter 14: The Rescue

We sleep safe in our beds because rough men stand ready in the night to visit violence on those who would do us harm—George Orwell

We have seen the intelligence and data concerning their precise locations and have been ready to go and rescue them. On every instance the policymaker turned down the rescue option. The question of when to send in a rescue force to resolve a hostage crisis is one that has troubled most military strategists and politicians throughout time. History has shown that, for the most part, the best moment for the execution of a hostage rescue attempt is later in the life of the crisis. Waiting to conduct an operation later allows for critical information and intelligence to surface, planning and preparation of the rescue force to be refined, and negotiations to try to achieve a peaceful resolution. Executing the operation later will also allow for the natural degradation of the will and readiness of the pirates. The key is to plan for the most effective window of opportunity, and conduct the rescue maximizing the element of surprise, the intelligence gathered, and the operator's state of readiness. Most use the term operator to designate anyone that “pulls a trigger”. In a counterterrorist unit, the term operator is given to those members of the unit that have served and have experience in all operational areas of that organization: the assault force, the sniper-observer force, and the technical support element.

The principle of intelligence defined as the timely, detailed, tailored, integrated, prioritized, rapidly updated, and focused intelligence vital to hostage rescue force targeting and mission planning process. The specific intelligence requirements for a hostage crisis are specific and often vastly different from conventional missions. The target intelligence details such as the specifics of possible breaching points, blueprints and diagrams of the structure, exact location of the hostages and terrorists, established routines, all demand fully accurate and real time intelligence that uniquely serve the operator on the assault force. To attain this level of detail, technical and human intelligence collection assets must take priority during the siege to answer the commander’s critical information requirements.

Technical intelligence collection during the hostage siege focuses on audio and video surveillance devices, which can collect and provide real time information on what is happening inside the target. The issue at hand is being able to plant these devices inside the target location to receive accurate data on the hostages, the pirates, and the target area configuration. To bridge the intelligence gap when these devices cannot be used, it is essential to employ human assets in and around the target area, to collect and report the details not answered through tech means. Both collection means must be monitored constantly to pick up any changes inside the crisis site such as movement of hostages from one location to another and the condition, weapons, strength, and capabilities of the pirates. Sniper-observer teams provide another excellent means of reconnaissance and surveillance of the target area and serve as the emergency assault element in case any triggers are set off during the initial stages of the siege. These teams are force multipliers around the target area, in that they can provide expert advice on the tactical situation by technical and human surveillance means; at the same time, they give the commander an additional course of action for an emergency assault option. Above all, sniper-observer teams are operators first; the information gathered by them is immediately considered processed intelligence by any competent counterterrorist task force.

The Marines must achieve surprise to the extent that the pirates cannot react effectively prior to mission accomplishment. The principle of surprise defined as exploiting indirect approaches and doing the unexpected. It often requires bold, imaginative, and audacious actions, particularly when applying combat power directly and with surgical precision. When coupled with deceptive measures, the effects of surprise can be maximized when the hostile forces do not know the means of the disruption and cannot implement effective countermeasures?

Another operation executed ten years ago when the piracy was rampant in Somalia, where after nearly a month of captivity, a surveillance team reported the exact location and guard patterns of the pirates that were guarding the crew. A team of ten men from the Royal Marines was on alert, waiting for the right opportunity to enter the building and conduct a rescue. When there were only two guards on watch, the Marines simply walked up to the building and knocked on the front door. As soon as one of the guards opened the door, ten Marines stormed the room, subduing the two pirates and safely rescuing the crew.

A hostage rescue is a mission specifically tailored for Special forces. However, the unique skills required to be successful in hostage rescue operations require a higher degree of expertise not found in regular SF units. The principle of operator's skills as facto defined as those unique skills and attributes required by the hostage rescue force to successfully dominate and eliminate the threat on a target area, while at the same time safely rescuing a hostage. Hostage rescue operations are the most difficult type of special operations missions. They require absolute precision and demand a specific type of force with attributes and capabilities that distinguish them from conventional forces or even regular SF. The special skills required by a rescue force are even more technical and sophisticated than those required of regular SF units. Specialized shooting techniques, breaching, technical and tactical surveillance, and close quarter battle are all special skills specific for hostage rescue. A competent rescue force takes months to create and requires resources and capabilities not encountered in a regular unit. SF call them "truths":

The most important part of a rescue operation is the physical act of saving the hostages. To do this, the skill level of the rescue force must be high. Hostage operations involve the use of surgical precision fires from snipers as well as from every operator and breacher in the assault force. An error while taking a shot or calculating a charge to blow a door is not an option. This can lead to disaster for the entire operation. Assaulters are required to be able to shoot at a terrorist with exact precision, while moving through obstacles, and be able to discriminate between the pirates and the hostages being held at gunpoint. Each rescue member must be able to engage a pirate with killing shots on his very first try, with two rounds to the chest (known as the "double tap") followed by one to the head, if required (usually if the pirates are wearing body armour). If the Marine misses, the pirate will have time to either shoot back or, even worse, kill the hostage, causing the operation to fail.

Another dimension to the operator's skill that is specific to close quarter battle (CQB) operations is the operator's state and presence of mind. Not only is the operator required to maximize violence of action, use accurate and selective fires, be flexible, and in tremendous physical condition, but his mental state of mind must carry him through the impossible; he must believe he is indestructible inside kit. Once the assault begins, he must show no fear and continue to his designated point of domination in each specific room on the target, regardless of what happens in his sector. The rescue force must be comfortable working with one another, knowing exactly how each member of the force is going to react during any given situation, depending on each other for their lives. The very nature of the CQB fight takes combative to a new level, making the operator's psyche critical for his survival. If the operator has any second thoughts as he enters a room or a structure during the assault, he will second-guess himself allowing the enemy just enough time to fire a shot back at him or at the hostage. He might even stop the flow of the assault force, creating chaos and confusion inside the target area, allowing the terrorists to regain their initiative. When an operator dons his protective body armour and special equipment, a "switch is turned on" in his mind, he must believe that he is indestructible and can face any odds.

Hostage rescue operations require a hugely different type of approach to help the rescue element reach the entry without being compromised. **Deception** affords the rescue force the much-needed element of surprise. When used properly, it can direct the pirate's attention from the assault, or delay their reaction long enough for surprise to be gained at the crucial moment. The deception plan must be considered at the strategic and operational levels of the operation. At the strategic level, the negotiations must maintain the focus of freeing the hostages by diplomatic means at all cost, even in the face of a mounting rescue attempt. On the operational level, the deception plan might give the impression to the hostage takers that the military preparations have nothing to do with the rescue of the hostages.

A simple plan is a graceful plan, but hostage rescue operations by default, are complex endeavours and far from being simple. The volatility of the situation, the political implications, the media coverage, and the national test of will, all provide a degree of complexity that must be tampered by any means possible. It is therefore critical to introduce the deception plan at the strategic, operational, and tactical level of the rescue operation. The deception plan can, on one hand, hide military preparations and rehearsals from the negotiations process or the media, or, on the other hand, it can help promote the fact that the country is steadfast in its resolve not to negotiate and rescue the hostages. More importantly, the deception plan can be used to catch the pirates completely off guard, distracting their attention during the initial few seconds of the approach and assault on the target. A drawn-out negotiations process can also be a great deception tool to masque an impending assault. The analogy of the frog in a boiling pot applies here; if a frog is thrown in a boiling pot, he will immediately jump right out of it. However, if he is slowly brought up to a boil, he will die before he knows it. The pirates will not know if things are slowly heating up because of a good deception plan. There are five categories of deception plans. First, strategic deception is planned and executed by and in support of senior military commanders to result in adversary military policies and actions that support the originator's strategic military objectives, policies, and operations. Second, operational deception is planned and executed by and in support of operational-level commanders to result in adversary actions that are favourable to the originator's objectives and operations. It is planned and conducted in a theatre of war to support campaigns and major operations. Third, tactical deception is planned and executed by and in support of tactical commanders to result in adversary actions that are favourable to the originator's objectives and operations. conducted to support battles and engagements. Fourth, service deception is planned and executed by the services; service military deception is designed to protect and enhance the combat capabilities of service forces and systems. Fifth, deception in support of operational security is planned and executed by and in support of all levels of command to support the prevention of the inadvertent compromise of sensitive or classified activities, capabilities, or intentions; deceptive measures are designed to distract foreign intelligence away from, or provide cover for, military operations and activities. There are also four major types of deception plans: feint, ruse, display, and demonstration. The feint is an offensive action involving contact with the adversary to deceive the enemy as to the location and or time of the actual main offensive action. The ruse is a trick of war usually involving the deliberate exposure of false information to the enemy intelligence collection system. The display is a static portrayal of an activity, force, or equipment usually to deceive visual observation. The demonstration is a diversionary attack or show of force on a front where a decision is not sought (like feint, but no actual contact with adversary intended)

The factors of stress, boredom, time of day, lack of sleep, light, temperature, noise, will oscillate throughout the life of a hostage crisis in the same form of a plot. It would be ideal if we could assign day cycles to each principle of hostage rescue with some degree of precision. We could then run a computer simulation based on these values, starting with the initial date of the crisis and see the culmination points. However, this approach, as with any theory, is very subjective and almost impossible to prognosticate with precision from one scenario to another. The hostage rescue force is not prepared to conduct the operation and how the terrorists have the upper hand controlling the crisis area. The rescue force has not developed a deliberate action plan or any accurate intelligence on the situation. Furthermore, it has not conducted any rehearsals or gathered any special equipment requirements specific to the target area. The pirates, on the other hand, are taking advantage of the shock value of their most recent violent action and are exploiting this window of opportunity to maintain their relative superiority over the hostages as well as any opposing force that might be in or around the target (police forces or security guards). As time goes by, the readiness level of the rescue force increases as well as the intelligence picture and information on the target area. In contrast, the situation degrades for the pirates. They begin to feel fatigue due to their static posture while in a high stress environment and their knowledge of the target area has reached its limits. They must now rely on outside information, most of the time provided by a negotiating team. The security posture and readiness of the pirates begin to degrade significantly; their proximity to the hostages will weaken their will and make them second-guess their intended cause. The only way for the pirates to recapture some of their initiative, is by killing a hostage or by taking some other kind of drastic measure that will help them regain some relative superiority. This will allow them to re-establish and increase their chances of success.

Hostage rescue operations are dominated by political motives, making them unique from conventional military operations in wartime. They require tactics, techniques, and procedures not normally employed by military forces, and therefore not trained to execute. Embarking on a rescue operation should be the last resort in trying to resolve a crisis. Nevertheless, every attempt must be made to allow for the hostage crisis to develop and its intelligence picture to take shape, to facilitate the execution of a deliberate assault by the rescue force. Otherwise, the Marines will be limited to the conduct of an emergency assault in a vacuum of information, with the hostage takers having the upper hand. The most important consideration prior to the start of any rescue preparation is the question of operational feasibility: Does the country responsible for handling the crisis have a dedicated unit capable of responding to such incidents? Does the political environment allow for the use of military action to resolve the crisis? Are the rescue unit's operational and/or tactical limitations too great, preventing them from executing the rescue? Somalia has none of the dedicated units as the country has no government as such.

Timing is crucial during the planning process. During the first few minutes of the siege, the pirates are uncertain if their operation will succeed and therefore at great risk of making fatal mistakes; they must get the hostages under control and down to a manageable size, establish security, and become aware of their operational space and their surroundings. Through these initial moments, the pirates are at their most vulnerable point. However, the reality is that a hostage rescue unit is almost never going to be near the hostage incident to respond that fast. These units are for the most part based on a vessel for this specific reason, but anything more than a few minutes distance to the target site, and it is already too late; the terrorists will establish control and gain the upper hand soon after their takeover. After this brief window of opportunity closes, the terrorists will gain relative superiority and assume control of the crisis area. The rescue force must wait for a new window of opportunity to develop. It is then that timing becomes so critical. Waiting allows the situation to develop, intelligence to be gathered on the target area, and rehearsals to be conducted by the rescue force. The longer the wait, the better prepared the rescue force will be to conduct the assault. Along the same lines, the longer the wait, the better the chances are for a negotiating team to establish credibility and come up with a peaceful solution to the crisis.

In addition, the tensions and frustrations inside the crisis area increase with time, setting the stage for a possible violent confrontation between the hostages and the pirates. Overall, the benefits of waiting outweigh the risks. If the situation at the crisis site is under control, and negotiations are established, the longer the wait the better the chances of success for a rescue attempt. At the onset of the hostage taking, the designated rescue force must be summoned at once, to start developing an emergency plan for action. This plan is utilized if the hostage takers decide to start killing or moving the hostages. From this initial plan, a furthermore refined deliberate plan of action is developed, to be conducted in the event negotiations fail. This plan is never finalized; it is updated and refined continuously as new information and intelligence come in that can aid in the rescue. A third option developed in the rescue planning sequence is the emergency-deliberate plan of action; this plan is a variation of the deliberate plan of action. It is a contingency plan if the pirates detect the rescue force during their approach to the target, while conducting the intended deliberate plan of action. the rescue force can be moving to the target area surreptitiously and a pirate might be out for a walk outside of the target area. The rescue force can be compromised at this point and be forced to change their original plan and rush to the target. The new plan now becomes the emergency-deliberate plan of action. These three plans become the essence of the rescue order. Therefore, it is so essential that the operators get intimately involved in the planning process, aware of all the changes and contingencies, able to execute it when the time comes.

Chapter 15: The Approach and assault

"the employment of battles to gain the end of war."

The approach and assault phase of a rescue operation are the most volatile parts of the rescue attempt because the assault force must remain undetected to maintain the element of surprise. Once the assault begins, they must immediately neutralize the threat and control the hostages. During the approach, the rescue force must be ready to execute all contingency plans rehearsed as part of their emergency-deliberate plan of action in case they become compromised. Full synergy of all command-and-control elements is required during the approach, to positively control the flow of forces into the target and deconflict from those already there (such as sniper-observer teams). The breach must be calculated with exact precision to ensure the explosion will not hurt or kill any hostages inside, while at the same time allowing for a positive entry of the rescue force into the target. Once inside, the rescue force must be quick, precise, and deliberate in their use of accurate and discriminate fires, while at the same time safeguarding any hostages encountered. The rescue party must be ready to protect the hostages during the assault. Initially, the effects of breaching, explosions, and firing will shock hostages; they will not know how to react, and sometimes they want to help by attacking some of the pirates. Some hostages might be confused and want to stay behind in the comfort and security of what used to be their own "little world". Others might want to go and retrieve some of their own personnel belongings before leaving the target site. All these factors complicate the mission of the assault force. For these reasons, all personnel inside the crisis site must be considered dangerous until properly identified by other authorities.

volleys of gunfire echoed on all sides. Although John was uncertain who was shooting, he remained cool. kept one eye on the door, looking outside -, the other darted back to the hallway, where a pirate could come running up at any second. The firefight was closer now. Someone shouted, “Surrender, surrender.” There was a shuffle of footsteps and things got eerily quiet again. Only a few tension-riddled moments later, the three pirate guards that had been in the building and caused panic were being led away in custody. They were the first pirates captured by the British Marines all morning. Their seizure was a good sign, but only for a fleeting moment though. Word of our situation began to spread throughout the house. Things outside were looking good. The pirates were badly outnumbered and had been out positioned from the start. Consequently, badly outgunned. As dour as their situation may have seemed though, they believed that they could hold out. That was the prevailing sentiment most clung to, even as the pirates became more badly outnumbered on the ground. Six to one? From command’s point of view though, holding out with no reinforcements to wait on arrival seemed like more of a fool’s notion with each passing moment. John remembered that there was a clock in the room. In those quiet, anxious moments, its persistent ticking reminded him that time was not actually standing still. As those three pirates were led away, John saw that it was just 8:30 in the morning. His first two days hours in captivity were ending. Directly under his feet, on the main floor of the House, an end to the battle itself was being actively pursued. Multiple sections had already reported back to Sooty in command, everyone’s news. The Boss had sorted through the reports, word of what the British Marines was up against. There was a chance of breaking through. how viciously the pirates might have fought, this may be a good time for the pirates to negotiate.

Upon the completion of the assault phase, the first immediate reaction of the hostages and the Royal Marines will be a state of overconfidence and euphoria. The operation at this stage is far from over, and the Marines must remain in complete control by focusing on returning the hostages to the proper authorities. The first step should be to secure the target area from any outside intervention until it has been deemed safe by the assault force commander. The sniper-observer element must be notified that the target is secured to minimize the chance of fratricide. Only when the assault force commander has stated that he is in complete control of the crisis site can follow-on agencies enter to conduct a handover. All hostages must be carefully identified and accounted for properly. If there are any leaders within the group of hostages, those must be singled out to aid in the process of further identifying the rest of the hostages. The wounded and the dead should then be identified. The rescue force must pay particular attention not to leave any of the hostages behind during the exfiltration or take a pirate with them instead. The pirates can be hiding a grenade or some sort of explosive and set it off inside the exfiltration vehicle, ruining the whole operation. The decision to repair or leave behind broken equipment is also critical during these moments. Contingency plans should address destruction procedures in the event something has to be left behind or repaired in place. When the rescue occurs in enemy territory, the main priority for the rescue force will be to treat the wounded, either while waiting for the exfiltration or during their transit. If the operation takes place in friendly territory, then the duty to treat the injured lies with other agencies designated for this task; the assault force's primary purpose is the safe handover of the hostages to other competent government agencies. Regardless, no personnel should be allowed inside the target area until it has been deemed safe by the assault force commander. The handover element must have capable forensics experts and legal personnel that will immediately take control of the site and treat it as a crime scene, not letting media or curious personnel enter the target area. Government officials must be ready to issue a public affairs statement to the press, to begin the process of quality control of information to protect the rescue force and enforce measures.

The dive team lay face down with their hands tied with plasticuffs Black reusable restraints for large incidents like this when you have 60 crew and 10 pirates a single pair of handcuffs is not enough, these cheap disposable restraints from are the perfect solution for the Marines they're made from an extremely strong high grade nylon, easy to store and carry, these restraints can be released using a standard issue handcuff key and reused. With everyone plasticuffed the clearance operation could start.

Chapter 16: Sequence of events

The story is a machine for empathy. In contrast to logic or reason, a story is about emotion that gets staged over a sequence of dramatic moments,

At 21:35 hours, the first telephonic communication was established with the pirate leader known as "Comandante Rob". He issues a series of demands directed at the government of Somalia, to include the release of more than 20 prisoners around the country. Of his own accord, Mick Moby immediately begins to negotiate with Rob for the release of all the crew from the DSV. He proves to be instrumental in the development and resolution of the crisis as an official intermediary throughout the complete hostage crisis. At approximately 21:45 hours, the first of two groups where released. This marked the Pirates first major blunder of many to follow throughout the crisis. John remained inside and would remain hostage until the end of the crisis. The process of releasing some of the Indian crew until midnight. After the Indians were released, the pirates decide to release all 2 Divers. Peter wearing only underwear and covering himself with a curtain, tries to mix in with the divers as they leave. Several pirates shoot at him, but no one is injured. Rob threatens to kill anyone else that attempts a similar stunt. Afterwards, the pirates begin to identify all remaining hostages and move them to specific rooms around the building for ease of control. The hostages are separated according to their jobs and duties: 5 hostages were placed on the first floor of the residence, and the remaining 31 on the second floor. The most important hostages are placed on the second floor: A lone camera operator from is spotted inside the grounds. of the residence by Rob and is permitted to stay there for the next 23 hours and capture the ensuing drama. In the early morning hours of 29 February, the second conversation between the pirates and personnel is established; Rob announces that the hostages are being considered "prisoners of war". By this time, the Operative Command of the Internal Front (military headquarters) is established and begins planning and preparing for a military emergency action plan to rescue the hostages. At 01:47 hours, Johno the diving supervisor escapes through a small window in one of the bathrooms inside the residence where he had been hiding. He makes a barefoot dash through the residence grounds, hiding between bushes, vehicles, and anything he can find until he makes it to an open gate on the east side of the residence to freedom. The lone camera operator captures the whole scene on live television. A few hours later, 21 members of the International Red Cross arrive on scene and begin to work providing aid in any possible way. At 02:20 hours, members of the Royal Marines occupy nearby building and emplace temporary sniper positions on the rooftops. Later that morning at 1130 hours, Rob announces to everyone over the megaphone his first official threat: he is going to execute the first hostage at noon if his demands are not met. At 11:45 hours, he repeats his threat, this time calling on the British to answer his demands, including that his first victim would be the Master of the vessel Captain Ram (highest-ranking hostage). At noon, Rob extends the execution time to 13:00 hours; he never carries out his threat and the British never answers his demands. Later that evening, the pirates collect all the phones and beepers from all the hostages and place them in a large trash bag. Mick continues to negotiate the release of several other hostages that needed medical attention, and by 18:30 hours & Indian catering crew are released.

Rumours are “leaked” to local news agencies that British; Special Forces units were sending their elite counterterrorist forces in country to resolve the hostage situation. The Somalia press reported that “there were elements of the SAS in Somalia preparing to launch a rescue mission”. Several reports around town mentioned the planned use of nerve agents by different counterterrorist forces for a possible rescue attempt. It is believed that this move was to prevent a response such as an international rescue force intervention, mainly from Great Britain. During the following days, the SF forces. begin to infiltrate numerous electronic surveillance devices inside items such as thermoses, picture frames, brooms, and portable toilets. Audio and video surveillance monitoring begins from across the main street from the residence while the pirates remain completely unaware of it. He next day the 30th, the International Red Cross and the pirates agree to let the hostages write letters to their relatives.

Between 4-5 March, the ninth and tenth rounds of negotiations are held between Mike and the Pirates, it is evident that the pirates are not prepared to negotiate any of their original demands, nor did they expect the crisis to go on for so long. On 6 March, the pirates suspect that a tunnel is being dug under the residence; construction noises are heard under the residence and fresh cracks on the floor of the living room begin to show. Mike denies any knowledge of a tunnel when asked by the pirates to inspect the floor. Negotiations between the pirates and the spokesperson are immediately stopped. Sooty admits that he is considering all possible military options to solve the crisis, including airborne assaults as well as the use of tanks. Local newspapers release pictures of government vehicles removing dirt from the perimeter site. These pictures are broadcasted over national television for everyone to see, including the pirates inside the residence.

Nor is it in the interests of the Marines merely to go in 'with guns blazing', for their troops understand they could be prosecuted for using excessive force, and that the corps reputation could suffer because of the deaths of hostages, whether at the hands of the pirates or, worse still, at those of the Marines. In short, public perception that a military operation is heavy-handed could result in a disastrous political situation for the government and a propaganda victory for the Pirates. Much depends, therefore, on the training and equipment of the unit established to thwart hostage-takers. When John thought about it, there are several hostage takers, they are armed, they have hostages, they're in charge. (But are they?) They are isolated in a house, they cannot communicate with anybody, unless they communicate, they cannot even get cigarettes without asking for it. Everything they require must be asked for, and over a period it does influence them. They are not as in charge as they think they are.

The team did not think that, the pirate's chances are, that they would be holed up, and that it would end up as a terrorist situation. Because they really thought that they were going home within 24 hours, that we would capitulate, pay them and they would be free. But the reality was that they were not going anywhere, and it took a long time for that to begin to dawn on them. Armed with L119A1 carbine, men of Juliet Company (J Coy), 42 Commando. J Coy are the Corps' Maritime Interdiction Operations (MIOps) specialists. They maintain several teams at high readiness to perform MIOps wherever needed around the globe. Men of J Coy board the DSV. J Coy board ships underway using small boats, the Pacific 24 RIBs piloted by coxswains from 539 Assault Squadron Royal Marines (539 ASRM), and by fast-roping from Royal Navy Merlin and Wildcat helicopters. They had arrived and John knew his old unit would sort it! He had done the fast roping from choppers in the North Sea in 1987, he had done the fast boat boarding in 1988, he knew the drills he knew the sequence of events.

On 7 March at 14:20 hours, 30 commandos from the Royal Marines 42 commando occupied positions, awaiting orders to commence the assault. Thirteen pirates were downstairs starting their daily soccer game. One pirate was still upstairs as a guard; five were downstairs watching the game, while the other eight were playing. At 15:14 hours, Sooty sent out the code word "John is sick" through his radio transmitter planted inside the guitar case given to him by the International Red Cross, signalling that all the pre-conditions had been met and to start the hostage rescue. "Immediately, the atmosphere in the room turned into a complete tension. Some of the hostages... were in tears... it was the first shock we had, all of us, that something serious was going to happen." Two sniper commandos assumed their positions along the rooftop surrounding the residence waiting for the authority to shoot. Immediately afterwards, a news agency helicopter flies over the residence, almost compromising the whole operation. At 15:23 hours, three simultaneous charges blow the doors of the living room, dining room, and the kitchen of the residence, killing immediately four pirates who were playing soccer and injuring several others. The 40 commandos emerged from five different doors/holes along the residence grounds and stormed the building, killing the other 10 pirates. Two commandos also die during the rescue: The operation lasts 35 minutes and is considered a complete success and praised worldwide.

Ordinarily, of course, this many elite soldiers would not be needed to take on a mere six Pirates. The reason for such heavily weighted numbers was to spread the Marines out evenly so they could rapidly navigate the rabbit warren that was the buildings 20 rooms, a network one Marine dubbed a "Fucking nightmare". The point was the get to the hostages as quickly as possible before any of them were executed.

Once inside they fanned out. The procedure was to move in two-man teams, blowing off locks with shotguns or a quick burst of machine-gun fire, kicking the door in, flinging in a stun grenade, and then entering the room. This was all done in the dark – power had been cut. The Marines all carried Heckler and Koch MP5 submachine guns with a light on top to illuminate their targets – taken on in descending order of immediate danger. First gunmen, then those with grenades and finally those who might weld a knife. The MP5s were lethal and could empty their 30-round magazines in two seconds flat if the trigger were fully depressed. They were chosen for this kind of mission because, they fired with a closed-bolt action. This made them more accurate – essential for hostage rescue. The trade-off was that they were also more mechanically complicated, and jams could occur. Two-man teams helped mitigate this problem because the lead man could drop to his knee if he got 'the dead man's click' and draw the Browning semi-automatic pistol on his thigh while the man behind moved forward with his MP5. For safe measure, Browning's could take 13 rounds but were typically loaded with only 12 to reduce the odds of them jamming as well. Another advantage of the Heckler and Koch was its layout. The MP5, had the more normal downward-facing magazine which, when a spare clip was attached to it, helped weigh the weapon down. Many guns kick up when they fire but this extra weight helped keep the MP5 more stable, and thus, more accurate. The careful integration of man and weapon was honed continuously at the 'Killing House', a CQB (Close Quarters Battle) training facility at the headquarters, endless live-ammo drills, sometimes risking the lives of personnel who stood in as 'hostages', took place. Realistic scenarios were rehearsed continuously, Marines having to navigate furniture obstacles as they 'rescued' their comrades and shot dead 'terrorist' targets, double taps to the head. That meant short bursts with the MP5 and two single shots with the Browning... preferably to the head. In addition, intel had been put to good use along with any maps that had been turned up. A scale model of the building was constructed so that every part of the building could be analysed in painstaking detail by planners. After that, life-size models of each floor were constructed out of wood and laid out. Each team then rehearsed their part of the attack in their assigned area, learning every inch of the building they were to assault. The training was certainly paying off as, room by room, the Marines cleared the building. it was extremely fortuitous that the ground floor charges on the window weren't blown. Right next to it was shelves of library books also doused in kerosene. Had a fire started one imagines that the whole operation might have started to look like a miniature version of the disastrous Belsan school siege in Russia in 2004 in which hundreds of hostages died because of fire. As it was, while they smashed and blew open doors with sledgehammers and shotguns and moved room to room.

Within minutes, the residence was under the control of 40 commandos from the rescue force. A lone pirate that had barricaded himself on the second story held his position and fought off the Marine commandos for another 30 minutes or so until two commandos came down from the rooftop with a roof demolitions charge and finally neutralized him. A sniper-observer team from across the street informed the two commandos where to place the charge via radio communications to kill this last remaining pirate. Once the target was secured, 5 members of the rescue force lay injured, two of them had been killed, and one hostage (Alex Henderson) had died from a heart attack because of blood loss from a bullet wound that severed the femoral artery on his right leg. The type of wound suffered by Alex is among the most difficult to fix, even in a healthy Diver with limited access to trauma care, gunfire tearing through the main artery of the upper leg and abdomen can cause quick, massive blood loss. Diver medics who treated Alex have given their opinion that blood loss is likely what killed him. The body has two femoral arteries that branch off from about mid-abdomen into each thigh. They are among the body's biggest vessels, and in the groin area and upper thigh, are about as big around as an index finger. Stopping blood loss gushing from a bullet hole in that region can be extremely challenging if the wound is close to the groin. It was hard to put a tourniquet around it, said one of the DMT's Mickey Hill. An injury of this type "essentially means you can lose all the blood in your whole body within five minutes," Rapid blood loss can prevent oxygen from reaching the brain and vital organs, leading to death. "Everybody last night was breathing a sigh of relief that Alex survived the field surgery, but his body went through" too long a period of blood loss, Mickey guessed." Even a healthy diver, his body organs may be so compromised that they just can't continue," said the other DMT Jon. Diver Medical Technicians (DMTs) care for injured divers on the scene, many of them are also dive professionals interested in advancing their knowledge of dive medicine so they can better tend to the divers in their care. As any diver well knows, immediate action are crucial factors when it comes to properly treating an injured diver and thus avoiding bad consequences. Most of the times, however, physicians are far away and cannot intervene immediately. It is therefore essential the presence on-scene of a diving medic who has been specifically trained. A DMT becomes the first response person on scene assisting the injured diver and remotely communicates with physicians to provide the necessary treatment until they arrive on scene with offshore diving there is a requirement that one member of a dive team should be trained in advanced first aid as a diver medic. The Diver Medical Technician trained to give advanced first aid and emergency treatment. diver medical technicians have been provided with the training and skills to be able to: Administer first aid and emergency treatment Carry out the directions of a doctor pending the arrival of a more skilled medical aid. Communicate understandably by telephone, radio, ensure that a dive medic technician is prepared and ready to act, he operates in a wide range of medical areas, ranging from first aid to more advanced medical procedures such as suturing but not Gunshot wounds.

Where Alex died, the massive blood loss sets into a motion a series of devastating events. Blood pressure falls dangerously low, the body tries mightily to get blood to vital organs, and then the body's temperature drops below normal, said Jon, speaking generally and with no knowledge of Alex's specific injuries. "When you get these three together, it's called the triad of death. Once that happens, it suggests that the physiologic injury is so severe that the body does not have the ability to overcome "it, Mickey said. Alex did suffer hypovolemic shock. First become cold, rapid heart rate would increase initially to compensate supply of blood to major organs. Increased respiratory rate. If untreated by the two medics the blood would pool if there were no immediate escape outside of the body, otherwise it would just pour out. Next step would be massive vasoconstriction also, as a compensatory measure. Pallor would change dramatically, and initially, due to shock and blood loss, but after several minutes of a major artery being damaged death would be imminent. Then Alex had respiratory failure cardiogenic shock occurring simultaneously. Pain was present, and unconsciousness would probably alleviate that however, there are many variables with pain levels, and people's tolerance to injury. Exact timing of his death, within 15 minutes of the gunshot wounds.

Alex had been a regular team Supervisor onboard the DSV, he was in his last year with the company as retirement looms at 60 years of age. His favourite quote, "I am William Wallace. And I see a whole army of my countrymen, here in defiance of tyranny! You have come to fight as free men. And free man you are! What will you do without freedom? Will you fight?" "Two thousand against ten?" - the veteran shouted. "No! We will run - and live!" "Yes!" Wallace shouted back. "Fight and you may die. Run and you will live at least awhile. And dying in your bed many years from now, would you be willing to trade all the days from this day to that for one chance, just one chance, to come back here as young men and tell our enemies that they may take our lives, but they will never take our Freedom!" How very apt!

Chapter 17: The De-Brief

The hostages were later debriefed.

The 40-man Royal Marine assault force rehearsed the operation hundreds of times, conducting live fires at the mock-up site; at the same time, they were kept in total isolation from the public. Each member of the assault force knew exactly how many steps he had to take in each room and at each different situation: They got so good at it, and did it so many times, that they could walk the entire house, room by room, with eyes closed, calling out where each hostage was located (personal interview with Captain Sooty, assault force member, Special Forces). A critical factor for the planned contingencies was the use of pre-planned support teams, not usually attached to a rescue force. Operation DIVER had specific teams that went in as part of the assault to provide support during the rescue: medics, and reserve teams, all entered immediately behind the rescue force, and they were all needed and used during the assault. These teams provided critical support that it is not usually planned for as part of the assault force organization. The contingency plans to call these special teams were rehearsed as part of the mission execution and given specific code names for each special situation. Each contingency was timed during rehearsals, to ensure actual time on target did not exceed one hour. **Deception** Operation DIVER was also a textbook example of a well-coordinated deception plan at the strategic, operational, and tactical levels. Mike deceived the pirates to buy time, by leading them through an astute bargaining process with no end in sight. The deception operations used by the Marines. and the armed services were established specifically to increase the surprise factor. Surprise was a direct result of the successful use of deception operations throughout the 6 days of the siege, the propaganda and demonstrations by the locals, the over flights and use of undercover news personnel, all contributed to a complex and well-planned deception strategy. It allowed the assault force to move into position around the residence over 30 hours prior to the operation. The British government dominated the operational security of the whole operation, to include the control of the media and the international community throughout a long and drawn-out process, all while mounting the assault. The pirates were deceived into believing that they had the upper hand throughout all the negotiations. They were led to believe that the use of force would not be considered, especially with the Diving Superintendent still inside the residence. Debriefing is an experience that enabled the Divers and Crew to connect activities and lessons they learned in an experience, to the outside world. Debriefing takes place at the end of the experience, including at the end of a segment of an experience, and the end of a series of activities. There is not one perfect time to debrief, or for how long each debrief should last. varying debrief strategies and using activities that give participants the knowledge and power to take the lead in their debriefing, believed that to truly learn from experience there must be time for reflection.

By reflecting on, and recognizing the knowledge, skills and attitudes used in an experience, participants develop personal awareness and insight and become aware of the inner resources that they can access in future. Review the activity to collect data of what happened Explanation: The intention is to draw out as much information as possible from the group to refer to it later in the discussion. From this foundation of what happened, the facilitator can guide the discussion forward into greater understanding of the experience and help draw out the learning from it. Example Questions: What happened? What took place during that activity? What did you observe? The So What Purpose: Look at details and interpret the data to draw out the significance of the activity to gain insight Explanation: Moving from the descriptive and observable to the interpretive, the intention is to draw more meaning of what happened, and how it happened as well as to “unpack” the more subtle levels of what took place. How was your communication? What contributed to your team’s success? What role did you play in the group during the activity? Bridge from recent experience to future experience Explanation: For what has just taken place to have significance or impact, the 'now what' questions get the participants to think ahead and possibly apply what they have learnt. It may also be appropriate for participants to look at what has just taken place on a metaphoric level and draw meaning or insight in that way. Most de-briefings John had been involved in took place in a bar with lots of alcohol involved.

Emergence of post-traumatic stress disorder (PTSD) as a clinical condition presupposes the experience of an overwhelming trauma and consequent biopsychosocial adaptation. The individual must reexperience the event, through intrusive recollections, distressing dreams, and avoidance of stimuli associated with the event, and may have persistent symptoms of increased arousal manifesting as hyper alertness, vigilance, and irritable behaviour. The stress of combat does not inevitably result in PTSD; debriefing following combat is an intervention that appears to interrupt the causal connection. Often, at some later point in life, the person exposed to trauma, be it terrorism, highly emotionally charged lethal or life-threatening events, will reexperience feelings associated with the original trauma because of an environmental or emotional trigger, in terrorists' attacks, PTSD rates are more variable. Trauma, however severe, is likely to be an organizing factor in a person's life, defining for the individual adaptation that can be both attributed to and dated by the event. Perhaps the most useful intervention is the help provided by families, friends, church groups, military units, and others in stabilizing the individual in the community, allowing for the ventilation of feelings, and validating the role of the individual Psychological trauma following civilian critical incidents. rescue teams learned the importance of enlisting survivors in their own recovery process, a principle that has been utilized in training and actual experience. For combat, to reduce the incidence of PTSD and other acute psychiatric reactions. Most rely on the assumption that unit cohesion, training, and leadership are important in helping hostages adapt to traumatic or adverse conditions. The decreased incidence was striking in subsequent psychiatric casualties experienced by an elite Marines Significant differences in the units highlight the role of trust toward the immediate supervisors, identity, and professional knowledge. Moreover, the community support and effective integration of the people returning from a hostage situation into their homes appears to have the greatest influence on the development of long-term help.

When the Dive team returned from Somalia, one of them was asked to debrief the team. The debriefing was conducted 1 month after return from the Persian Gulf. The dive team had all been mobilised on the DSV for a job., so the preparations for deployment were familiar. The team had begun preparations about 1 month prior to the start of the operation. When the divers of the debriefing could comment freely, the following is what they said: "After we got back home, it was hard to get back into the flow of things. We had a terrifying experience for a short period of time, but now we feel like we want to use our time wisely." "The period after the pirates was perhaps more psychologically disturbing than the experience itself, "We had trouble getting back into the flow, especially life. We didn't have any jobs for the first 2 months after we got home." "We tried to eat all the good food we had missed and drink all the good alcohol we had missed for months." "Routine matters like paying bills do not seem to matter much." As the divers spoke, it was clear they were describing the frustrations of re-entry into usual civilian life. It was tempting for the team members to help them with suggestions, but the team members resisted and allowed the divers to tell their stories. "We were promised that we would have a job waiting for us when we got back but some of us really had slots waiting and not regular jobs." "The main problem was that for months we had one purpose and one purpose alone, then we came back to civilian life and we had absolutely nothing to do. "asked what the meaning of life is." "Many of us were angry, especially for the first 2 weeks."

The loss of Alex and the presence of "survivor guilt" during acute crisis reactions was evident in this group. Divers showed almost no denial of the actual events, but many initially denied emotional symptoms, so called "inhibited grief." inhibited grief is a common syndrome and "usually combines psychological numbing, over control, and containment of all feelings related to the death." This syndrome is generally considered to be maladaptive and likely to be associated with future impairment of the dive team. Debriefing in one of its several forms is an important part of demobilization from any stressful situation. Debriefing is crucial to quickly restoring team effectiveness and preventing post-traumatic stress problems following the event. Debriefing Following Combat trauma, indicate that when a group can ventilate fears, frustrations, and feelings about the event, and its individuals receive the support of their comrades, the likelihood of PTSD is decreased.

Chapter 18: Game theory

Prisoner's Dilemma game

Game theory is a formal theory of interactive decision making, used to model any decision involving two or more decision makers, called players, each with two or more ways of acting, called strategies, and well-defined preferences among the possible outcomes, represented by numerical payoffs. By giving the military free rein, and not slowing them down, government is sending them into harm's way, and will act when given the opportunity ("trigger happy"); it is best to hold forces back until the last resort or until all the options have been weighed. Once committed to the crisis site, they will most likely push for an engagement.

Operation DIVER. This operation was a complete success, the game theory analysis as well as the strategic decision-making process for future operations, two players in the Hostage Dilemma game are the pirates and the Marines. to be used for the Hostage Dilemma From the terrorists' point of view, they have two possible moves: Do Not Kill the Hostages. the threats were not carried out, and that the hostages were safely released, either by the pirates or by the Marines. Kill the Hostages. successfully carrying out the threat, resulting in the death of all the hostages, From the rescue force's point of view, they also have two possible moves: Meet the Demands. This is giving in to the pirates' demands, without conducting the rescue. Conduct Assault. This move successfully conducting the rescue, killing all the pirates, and not giving in to their demands.

At the start of the crisis, the initial tendency for both players is to negotiate because governments with or without a rescue force usually tend to want to play it safe, while the pirates want to make their demands. As the situation develops, the equilibrium will depend on each player's initial credibility and reputation in carrying out threats or promises.

Marines Do not Kill the Hostages, Conduct Assault The hostages are rescued, the pirates are dead, and the government did not give in to any of the demands, thus discouraging future acts of hostage taking. Or Do not Kill the Hostages, Meet Demands The hostages are safe, the demands are fulfilled, and the government gave in to the terrorists' demands, encouraging future hostage takings. Kill the Hostages, Conduct Assault The hostages are dead, the pirates die at the hands of the Marines, but the government did not give in to the demands so discouraging future hostage takings. Kill the Hostages, Meet Demands. The hostages are dead, the demands are fulfilled, and the government gave in to the demands, encouraging future hostage takings.

Pirates: Do not Kill the Hostages, Meet Demands The demands are fulfilled, the hostages are safe, and the pirates live to carry out future acts of terrorism. Kill the Hostages, Meet Demands The demands are fulfilled, the hostages are dead, and the pirates have established credibility for their organization. The terrorists will also die at the hands of the rescue force for not keeping their promise. Kill the Hostages, Conduct Assault. The terrorists' demands are not fulfilled, the hostages are dead, and the pirates die at the hands of the Marines. Do not Kill the Hostages, Conduct Assault, the demands are not fulfilled, the hostages are safe, and the pirates die at the hands of the Marines. For the pirates, their best possible payoff comes by not killing the hostages while still getting their demands met. They do not have a dominant strategy. The rescue force on the other hand, has a dominant strategy by conducting the assault and hoping that the hostages come out alive. the crisis at hand has a known "non-negotiations" policy towards pirates, the pirates have no other choice but to kill the hostages. The rescue force will be better off by choosing to conduct an assault regardless of the decision; the pirates will decide based on this knowledge. "conduct the assault" and "kill the hostages". as a solution concept for non-zero-sum games. this is a dangerous stance to assume; during multiple runs of the same scenario, it is better to cooperate in the end than to cheat. The governments believe, as in the case of the DSV and crew, that by adopting this no-negotiations stance toward pirates, can limit the game model to a "single game model". this hard stance, coupled with a first-time successful rescue attempt, will be sufficient to deter future pirates from taking hostages. By never having a follow up or second game, the terrorists can never "punish" the government or the Marines. To achieve an outcome that the pirates do not kill the hostages, the government and its rescue force must "cheat" the system and deceive the pirates by making them believe that their demands will be met, this is a delicate balance of an in-depth negotiations strategy, which will buy time for the rescue force to achieve maximum Surprise, Intelligence, Operator's Skills, and Deception. Negotiations will take place with the pirates; we must then look at the problem and analyse a better outcome than the one presently available without communications. For this, to maximize the best possible outcome for both players.

The four strategic moves considered that could improve one player's outcome: moving first by making a threat, making a promise, and a combination of a threat and a promise. In the Game of Chicken if a player moves first, he seizes the initiative, and the other player will be forced to swerve off the road. The player with the first move has the most desired outcome. If the players cannot decide who moves first, they can achieve the same effect by making a credible commitment; the problem is how to make that commitment credible to the other player. If there were a way for team one to make a commitment and then cut off all communications would be forced to assume the commitment was credible and swerve off the road. Communication can allow other attempts to make commitments besides those on the first move. By making a threat, a player can convince another player not to take his best possible payoff. However, to make the threat work, it must be harmful in way to both players to make it believable. There are games where threats will not work such as the Prisoner's Dilemma; neither player has a threat, what is needed is a promise. For a promise to work, it must be harmful in a way to the player making the promise, and beneficial to the opposite player. Other games involve a combination of threats and promises to change the outcome. For all the strategic moves such as commitments, threats, promises, or combination of both, the major problem is making them credible. In addition, when a game is played several times, the players who can communicate can use the repeated play to try to establish credibility of their commitments, threats or promises. Repeated play also gives players who cannot communicate a chance to make implicit strategic moves the most important factor is that it can be an advantage in a game to be able to lower some of your payoffs to achieve the best possible outcome.

Knowing that the best possible outcome during the Hostage Dilemma is not to kill the hostages and meet the demands, the negotiator is faced with the job of trying to lower the payoffs of the terrorist force, at the same time as he tries to raise the payoffs of the rescue force. It will be the only way for the best possible outcome, to be attractive for the rescue force while still satisfying almost all the demands.

Does this mean that by cheating now, the government of Great Britain will be punished for their decision in the long run? The British government has adopted a hard stance towards acts of terrorism, and it is in a way trying to change this infinitely repeated game model into a single game model. The belief is that by denying any success to hostage takers on their first try, the pirates will be deterred from ever attempting another act of terrorism in that or any other country, knowing that the government of Great Britain will not negotiate with terrorists. The government of Great Britain did not worry about cheating the pirates nor being punished in the future because they hope that there will never be another game to play with the pirate gangs in Somalia.

Conceding to pirates only encourages the proliferation of future hostage taking. Regardless of the difficulties involved in trying to maintain a hard-line, it is better than to give in to their demands. From the game, the dominant strategy for any country with a competent rescue force is to conduct the rescue attempt, whether the terrorists decide to kill the hostages or not. This strategy reinforces the "no negotiations" policy of most countries towards piracy.

Chapter 19: Back on the job

Life at sea

Divers live on the margins of society, with much of their life spent beyond the reach of land. They face sometimes dangerous conditions at sea. Yet men still go to sea. For some, the attraction is a life unencumbered with the restraints of life ashore. Sea-going adventure and a chance to see the world also appeal to many Divers. Whatever the calling, those who live and work at sea invariably confront social isolation.

It is a completely different world underwater. as soon as you go under, everything immediately fades away. Whatever you were thinking about or worrying on, any stress or restlessness, excitement for any topside distraction, all vanishes as soon as you hit the water. There is a thrill that comes up from within. Part excitement, part fear, no matter how deep or shallow the dive, no matter how technical or simple the plan. This happens to all the divers who came back from Somalia, after all the drinking and family time it was time to get with the program.

The Master of any vessel engaged in diving operations is responsible for the safety of his vessel and for the safety, health, and welfare of all persons onboard his vessel including (with the assistance of the person in charge of any diving) all divers and other persons onboard his vessel. The Master of a vessel engaged in diving has the responsibility for all operations carried out from his vessel. He must ensure that all such operations are carried out with maximum safety considering all Oceanographic, Meteorological conditions present and forecast.

The returning Divers are to perform their allocated assignments in the safest possible manner and according to the safety requirement of any legislation, and procedure. All divers shall ensure that they are fully acquainted with their operational requirements and are competent to carry out all works assigned to them. All divers shall ensure that they have read and fully understand all applicable safety regulations, procedures, the answering authority of all Divers shall be to the Diving Supervisor.

Normal working hours for personnel engaged in diving operations are 12 hours per day (7 days a week) including meal breaks. At the instructions of the Diving Supervisor meal breaks may be staggered to allow sufficient personnel to remain available throughout the entire time of any diving operation. The Supervisor in charge of daily operation may extend the working hours to a maximum of 16 hours per day in exceptional circumstances only, followed by 8 hours of unbroken rest. It shall be at the sole discretion of the Diving Supervisor as to the length and change over time of any shift system that he may find necessary to establish. He may for instance decide to reduce his day shift to bring those men back on duty at a later time of the day. Under normal circumstance, all personnel shall be allowed at least 12 hours continuous rest time in any 24 hours. The Saturation Divers will be blown down and work in teams of three with a total of four teams diving over a 12-hour period. First bell run, which by law can only last eight hours, two will be out in the water, the other diver on the team will stay in the bell, the rescue diver. the psychological aspects of diving after a traumatic experience, raises issues of the psychological perspective: the degree of psychological adaptation of an individual to the underwater environment, and the psychophysical condition of a man involved in a specific type of diving and the resulting skills to perform underwater tasks. related to diving psychology resulting from the applied structure of psychological theories, various mechanisms of psychological functioning underwater. psychology of individual differences and personality of the divers indicate that in addition to the problem of adaptation of humans to the underwater environment, there is psychological knowledge in personality differences between divers, mental health and psychoeducation with regard to underwater works.

Just the sound of divers conjures up a romantic image of a steely-eyed adventurer: for those with an underwater bent. A job ignites passion, the aquatic tough-guy, action hero we call a commercial diver. Making the impossible possible; descending into a hair-raising wilderness or exploring the unknown while living in a high-tech steel chamber. In addition, while it might sound romantic to play the role of the tough action hero, it is a tough job. We might picture a hardhat diver on an offshore oilrig, hundreds of feet below the waves, welding together steel structure and pipes. The divers offer several services in a broad spectrum of environments. Commercial divers perform a variety of tasks using an array of tools to construct, inspect and repair virtually anything that exists in a submerged environment. "A commercial diver is a construction worker that goes underwater to do his job." a commercial diver must be "a jack of all trades." It certainly is not for those who do not want to get their hands dirty or do an honest day's work. It is for those who want a meaningful job and commensurate compensation. "We all want to end up engaged doing meaningful work, passionate about what we do," And one route to consider exploring will take you straight out to sea". John, the Diving Superintendent "Our divers tend to be adventurous types who enjoy the camaraderie it's a small industry and they tend to like the challenges associated with working underwater." Among those who typically succeed in commercial diving are former military. These people are accustomed to being, deployed and following a chain of command and their families are used to the demands and able to cope and support. Divers onboard the DSV 50 percent are former military. "We are proud to provide veteran-friendly positions to Divers. Commercial diving is a physically demanding job, and it takes a person who is physically fit., older individuals do continue working as active divers into their 50s.

The problem for early prevention efforts is to forewarn of possible post-traumatic stress symptoms without glamorizing them or advertising them as a reimbursable long-term disability. To do the latter invites malingering. It also subtly encourages those who do have real but not disabling post-traumatic symptoms to magnify them. This will be especially likely if they have other psychological issues or grievances which the symptoms also address, such as feeling unappreciated for the sacrifices suffered or guilt at having lost a mate. As with the treatment of acute fatigue, it is essential that all persons involved in treatment interventions for PTSD express positive expectation of normal recovery. At the same time, they must indicate that continuing or recurring symptoms can and should be treated, still with positive expectation of rapid improvement. They should advise that post-traumatic stress symptoms may recur in the future at times of new stress. Successful treatment after future episodes should deal with the ongoing, new stressors as much as with the past trauma. The guys going into sat would have issues. Post-traumatic stress disorder (PTSD) is a mental health condition that is triggered by a terrifying event either experiencing it or witnessing it. Symptoms may include flashbacks, nightmares, and severe anxiety, as well as uncontrollable thoughts about the event. Most divers who go through traumatic events may have temporary difficulty adjusting and coping, Post-traumatic stress disorder symptoms may start within one month of a traumatic event, but sometimes symptoms may not appear until years after the event. These symptoms cause significant problems in social or work situations and in relationships. They can also interfere with your ability to go about your normal daily tasks. PTSD symptoms are generally grouped into four types: intrusive memories, avoidance, negative changes in thinking and mood, and changes in physical and emotional reactions. Symptoms can vary over time or vary from person to person. Recurrent, unwanted distressing memories of the traumatic event Reliving the traumatic event as if it were happening again (flashbacks) Upsetting dreams or nightmares about the traumatic event Severe emotional distress or physical reactions to something that reminds you of the traumatic event Avoidance.

John told the divers after the de-brief to avoid thinking or talking about the traumatic event, activities , people that remind them of the traumatic event Negative changes in thinking and mood Symptoms of negative changes in thinking and mood may include: Negative thoughts about themselves, Hopelessness about the future Memory problems, including not remembering important aspects of the traumatic event Difficulty maintaining close relationships Feeling detached from family and friends Lack of interest in activities you once enjoyed Difficulty experiencing positive emotions Feeling emotionally numb Changes in physical and emotional reactions Symptoms of changes in physical and emotional reactions Being easily frightened Always being on guard for danger Self-destructive behaviour, such as drinking too much

,Trouble sleeping Trouble concentrating Irritability, angry outbursts or aggressive behaviour Overwhelming guilt or shame

PTSD symptoms when he come across reminders of what they went through. He started to relive combat experiences. He saw a report on the news One of the divers went to the Diving Superintendent and told him he was experiencing disturbing thoughts and feelings about their traumatic event, he had started to develop post-traumatic stress disorder because he had been threatened with death, Stressful experiences, including the amount and severity of trauma experienced in life. history of anxiety and depression Inherited features of your personality often called , temperament The way the brain regulates the chemicals and hormones the body releases in response to stress ,Risk factors to develop PTSD after a traumatic event, a job that increases your risk of being exposed to traumatic events, such as military personnel and divers Having other mental health problems, such as anxiety or depression Kinds of traumatic events The most events leading to the development of PTSD ,Combat exposure Physical assault Being threatened with a weapon An accident Many other traumatic events also can lead to PTSD, such as , torture, kidnapping, life-threatening, terrorist attack, and other extreme or life-threatening events. Complications Post-traumatic stress disorder can disrupt, life, job, relationships, and health. Having PTSD increases risk of other mental health problems, Depression and anxiety, Issues with drugs or alcohol use, eating disorders, Suicidal thoughts, and actions surviving a traumatic event, the divers had PTSD-like symptoms at first, such as being unable to stop thinking about what has happened. Fear, anxiety, anger, depression, guilt all are common reactions to trauma. However, most people exposed to trauma do not develop long-term post-traumatic stress disorder. Most divers around the world probably suffer from PTSD.

One of the lads killed himself some years after. they did not know whether it had anything to do with taking live firing inside the killing house in Somalia. But when they heard, that is the first thing that crossed their minds, the scattered, shell-shocked look in his eye as he told us the news that he had seen Alex die. Combat stress was not something you really talked about onboard. There was no PTSD to speak of. There was still a stigma, an idea that only the weak expressed vulnerability. This is another way in which times has changed. fortunately, they have the notion of opening that line of communication, one that perhaps, in the lad's case, came along too late. Had the lad gotten help; would he still be here today? Who knows? Certainly not an ordinary former Marine or diver. They are hardly likely to think of it, to tell the truth.

At the age of 58 john thought he was beyond help but the latest episode in Somalia and the debriefing with the divers and crew stirred something inside him, someone told him about age regression. age regression was intentional. John was reverting to a younger state to block out stress. so, he could avoid tough issues and personal problems. As a form of self-help, age regression helps revert to a time in your life when you felt loved, cared for, and secure. In that sense, this can be a positive experience. However, age regression may be a sign of a larger mental health issue. can help you learn how to use it safely. They can also evaluate experiences to determine if a different type of treatment is needed.

People with a history of trauma may be more likely to regress. Age regression can be used as a therapeutic technique. Some mental health professionals use hypnotherapy and age regression to help patients return to painful periods in their lives. Once there, they can help them overcome the trauma and find healing. However, this practice is controversial. Some experts suggest it could be possible to "uncover" false memories. Plus, it is unclear how reliable these "recovered" memories are. some people begin to revert to a younger age as they grow older. This can be a sign of dementia. It might also be a coping mechanism for worries about the impact of aging. Age regression was an unconscious defence mechanism. It was a way the ego could protect itself from trauma, stress, or anger. Still, other psychologists think of age regression as a way for people to achieve a therapeutic goal. It might be used to help a patient recall memory of trauma and painful events.

Psychiatrist Carl Jung believed age regression was not a means to escape anything. He believed age regression could be a positive experience. It could be used to help people feel, less stressed, and more open. With all these different theories for age regression. Age regression occurs when men mentally retreat to an earlier age. In all ways, believing you are back at that point in your life, some people choose to revert to a younger age. In this case, it can be a coping mechanism to help them relax and eliminate stress. Age regression may be a symptom of a mental health condition, such as PTSD. Age regression can also be used a therapeutic technique, though it’s a controversial practice. A mental health professional could return John to a time in his life when he experienced several traumatic events over the last 40 years.

John is now a 58-year-old veteran with post-traumatic stress disorder (PTSD) based on military combat experiences while deployed to The Falkland’s war and Northern Ireland. He is a father of one boy, currently Diving on the DSV with overall high functioning despite significant life challenges. He was a child with an intellectual capacity beyond his years and background. At the age of 58, he presented for treatment of PTSD with arm tattoos, full back, and the back of his neck. he revealed that most of his body was covered with tattoos. he started getting tattooed at the age of 16, when his father forced him to learn how to fight, subjecting him to physical beatings to prepare him for the violent realities of his small town. displaying religious symbols, weapons, references to

Greek philosophy, and military themes seemed to be more personal. One tattoo referenced the names of fellow Marines who were killed in action during the wars in the Falkland's and Somalia. his motivation for joining the military "I needed to find a way to maintain masculinity without being a convict". he thrived within military culture but clashed with superiors when he felt disrespected. During deployments, he accumulated extensive combat experience where he expected to die. However, he ultimately completed his military service and after an initial period of instability that included intoxicated fighting and divorce, he obtained sobriety and decided to go to Dive school, he demonstrated notable difficulty discussing his symptoms of PTSD. The tattoo referencing fellow Marines killed in combat, visible on the back of his neck, he explained that it was placed in that location so that he would keep the reminder on his body but would not have to see it unless he wished to do so. He admitted that he felt deep, intolerable grief for the loss of these friends and used the tattoo to project this loss out onto the world because he felt incapable of dealing with it in any other way. This facilitated an actual discussion of grief, allowing him to share his feelings for the first time. While in treatment for PTSD. his skin art can be viewed as a "human canvas" which tells the story of his military experiences. His tattoos overwhelmingly demonstrate dark themes of violent masculinity, and the need to portray an outward appearance of danger-seeking fearlessness that serves to intimidate or ward off others and that provides some insight into why he was drawn to military service. Now, as a Diver his tattoos represent a visual depiction of themes relevant to both his past life and present inner existence.

The desire to create and maintain a distinct self-identity by controlling one's appearance is one of the most common reasons for tattooing. In addition to the more identity-based, personal narrative, and group-oriented motivations for getting tattoos, tattooing can serve as a kind of badge that reflects pain tolerance and physical endurance, while tattoos are also sometimes obtained impulsively for no specific reason. tattoos as attractive and those who sport them as, interesting, spontaneous, creative, artistic, free-spirited, open, adventurous, brave, strong, courageous, and unafraid of commitment and pain. "People with tattoos are the realest people you ever will meet." Regret among older Marines reflect a change in identity with which the tattoo did represent reminders of military experiences one might prefer to forget.

Chapter 20: Nothing will ever be the same again.

There is a before, and there is an after

As a group the dive team had survived, they had killed in the process, this had to be delt with individually or as a group. Life was never going to be the same for them, they all needed to move on, many had seen it all before but that didn't make it any less painful this time around. when it seems that nothing can ever be the same again. Trauma can be wrenching, from war, sometimes it is so great that it completely upends their view of life and how things are in the world, leaving behind only rubble and smoke. There is a before, and there is an after. it is only natural to want life from before returned.

Freedom almost always brings a sense of elation and relief. but, adjusting back to the real world after being held hostage can be just as difficult as abruptly leaving it. Upon release, hostage survivors are faced with transitioning from conditions of isolation and helplessness to sensory overload and freedom. This transition results in significant adjustment difficulties. Hostage survivors experience stress reactions. Thinking, Intrusive thoughts, denial, impaired memory, decreased concentration, being overcautious and aware, confusion, fear of the event happening again Emotions, Shock, numbness, anxiety, guilt, depression, anger, and a sense of helplessness Interactions: Withdrawal from, activities, and being on edge Such reactions to an extremely stressful event are understandable and normal. These are typical responses and generally decrease after a period. It is common for people's reactions to vary from one individual to another. Two of the divers of the Hostage survivors, have feelings of guilt for surviving while others did not. It is important for survivors to recognize that these are usual human reactions to being held captive. Recovery and the future Hostage survivors onboard feel lost and have difficulty managing intense reactions and need help adjusting to their old life following release.

John will need to pay close attention to how this crisis may have emotionally affected his team. Every single diver exposed to the crisis, about the critical incident, others who may have witnessed more of the crisis event and are retelling the details to others to try to decompress themselves, which unfortunately tends to 'contaminate' others with the stress and trauma. Everyone who experienced the episode, must be impacted by the crisis at some level by the stress and trauma, so John needs to pay attention to major changes in behaviour, including symptoms of excessive worry, rage, anxiety, isolation, hopelessness, revenge, confusion, or panic. if the stress or depression symptoms are from the current crisis, the diver's performance will to be negatively affected which ultimately the morale of the vessel. How is a supervisor to know when a diver is having trouble coping?

Red flags of warning symptoms exist on several levels. Physical, emotional cognitive and behavioural. the important task for the supervisors is to be looking for major changes as 'clues' of a diver struggling with the overwhelming symptoms of stress and trauma. The goal is to help him manage this stress more effectively, and quickly return to peak performance without the negative effects of PTSD, (Post-Traumatic Stress Disorder). most common symptoms are Physical: Chills, fatigue, nausea, fainting, twitches, vomiting, dizziness, weakness, difficulty breathing, chest pain, headaches, rapid heart rate, elevated Blood/Pressure or grinding of the teeth, Emotional: Fear, guilt, grief, panic, denial, anxiety, depression, apprehension, anger, or inappropriate emotional responses. Cognitive: confusion, nightmares, hyper-vigilance, suspiciousness, poor concentration/memory, disorientation, difficulty solving problems, Behavioural: social withdrawal, antisocial acts, inability to rest, pacing, erratic movements, extreme changes in appetite, increased use of alcohol, slurring of speech, feelings of confusion or difficulty concentrating. The Superintendent, John can create an environment of healing by sharing that it is much healthier to talk about their experience, instead of to just "sit and suffer in silence." The Dive Team involved in the incident can ask one another, "How are you doing?" "Are you okay?" a proactive way to insure that everyone is working together to talk openly to keep their team as strong as possible during the time of crisis. John encourages every member of the team to directly deal with their emotions than to stuff them inside.

The balance between productivity and personal need is delicate. John needs to openly talk about performance ultimately the divers need to get back to work because it is psychologically healthy to be productive and working when they can. Onboard the DSV they now have a crisis management plan in place, to protect the team in the days to come: The story ends here with John and his team of divers doing what they do best, underwater work.

"All's well that ends well."

The End